PRENTICE HALL

Choices

in LITERATURE

The Adventure of Me
Joining Hands
It's Up to You
Conflict and Resolution
The World of "What if . . . ?"

The Me You See
Where Paths Meet
Deciding What's Right
You Are the Solution
Communication Explosion

Myself, My World
American Tapestry
Justice for All
Making a Difference
Charting Your Own Course

Joining Hands

PRENTICE HALL
Upper Saddle River, New Jersey
Needham, Massachusetts

ISBN 0-13-411323-3

1 2 3 4 5 6 7 8 9 10   00 99 98 97 96

Cover: Student Art *Untitled*, Margaret Noel, Walt Whitman High School, Bethesda, Maryland

Art credits begin on page B146.

PRENTICE HALL
Simon & Schuster Education Group
A VIACOM COMPANY

Staff Credits for Prentice Hall Choices in Literature

(In Alphabetical Order)

Advertising and Promotion: Carol Leslie, Alfonso Manosalvas, Rip Odell

Business Office: Emily Heins

Design: Laura Bird, Eric Dawson, Jim O'Shea, Carol Richman, AnnMarie Roselli, Gerry Schrenk

Editorial: Ellen Bowler, Megan Chill, Barbara W. Coe, Elisa Mui Eiger, Philip Fried, Rebecca Z. Graziano, Douglas McCollum

Manufacturing and Inventory Planning: Katherine Clarke, Rhett Conklin, Matt McCabe

Marketing: Jean Faillace, Mollie Ledwith

Media Resources: Libby Forsyth, Maureen Raymond

National Language Arts Consultants: Kathy Lewis, Karen Massey, Craig A. McGhee, Vennisa Travers, Gail Witt

Permissions: Doris Robinson

Pre-press Production: Carol Barbara, Kathryn Dix, Marie McNamara, Annette Simmons

Production: Margaret Antonini, Christina Burghard, Greg Myers, Marilyn Stearns, Cleasta Wilburn

Sales: Ellen Backstrom

Acknowledgments

Grateful acknowledgment is made to the following for permission to reprint copyrighted material:

Robert Bly
"Friends All Of Us" by Pablo Neruda, from *Neruda and Vallejo: Selected Poems*, edited and translated by Robert Bly, Beacon Press, 1971, 1993. Copyright 1971, 1993 by Robert Bly. Reprinted with his permission.

Curtis Brown Ltd.
"Skybird to the High Heavens" by Nancy White Carlstrom is reprinted by permission of Curtis Brown Ltd. Copyright © 1990 by Nancy White Carlstrom. First appeared in *Light: Stories of a Small Kindness* published by Little Brown and Company.

Cricket Magazine
"Frosted Fire" by Sheila Kelly Welch is reprinted by permission of *Cricket* magazine, January 1994, Vol. 21, No. 5, © 1994 by Sheila Kelly Welch.

(Continued on page B146.)

Joining Hands
Contents

HOW DO WE CARE FOR ONE ANOTHER? B7

Looking at Literary Forms: Biography and Autobiography

WHAT ARE FRIENDS FOR? **B43**

Looking at Literary Forms: Folk Tales

HOW ARE WE DIFFERENT BUT REALLY THE SAME?

About This Program

What makes reading exciting?

Reading is a great way to learn more about the world and about yourself. Reading gives you the chance to make a movie in your mind and experience adventures you might never be able to actually live. Words can take you to faraway lands, tell you about important discoveries and courageous people, make you laugh and cry, or let you look at your world in a new way.

How will reading pay off in your future?

Beyond being entertaining, reading is important. As you learn more, you increase your choices in life. The skills and strategies you practice today will help you to become a life-long learner—someone who has questions, reads to answer them, and develops more questions!

How will this book help you get more out of what you read?

This book and your teacher will help you become a better reader. The selections included will grab your attention and help you practice specific skills valuable to the reading process.

Questions and activities at the beginning of selections will help you relate the reading to your own life; questions at the end will help you expand on what you learned. Activities and projects throughout the book will help you generate and explore new pathways of learning.

What features make this book a great learning tool?

• **Artwork to Spark Your Interest** Fine art, student art, photography, and maps can give you clues about the writing and direct the way you read.

• **Exciting Activities to Get You Into the Selection** A preview page for each selection asks a question to get you thinking. Stop and consider your own responses to this question. Talk with classmates to get their ideas. As you read, you may find your own opinions changing. Reading can do that, too.

 The **Reach Into Your Background** feature will always give you ideas for connecting the selection to your own experience. In many cases, you may know more than you think you do. Try the activities in this section for a jump start before you read. Don't expect to be in your seats all the time! You'll learn more about your ideas by role-playing, debating, and sharing what you know with others.

• **Useful Strategies to Help You Through the Selection** This program will teach you essential techniques for getting more out of your reading.

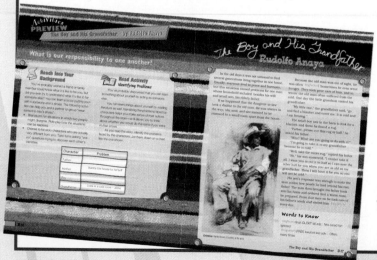

In **Read Actively** you'll find hands-on approaches to getting more out of what you read. Here's your chance to practice the skills that will bring you reading success. You'll learn to make inferences, gather evidence, set a purpose for reading, and much more. Once you've learned these skills, you can use them in all the reading that you do . . . and you'll get more out of your reading.

Some of the strategies you'll learn include:

> Identifying Problems
>
> Making Judgments
>
> Asking Questions
>
> Visualizing Characters
>
> Setting a Purpose for Reading
>
> Recognizing a Sequence of Events
>
> Connecting Nonfiction to Your Own Experience
>
> Responding to Literature

Activities MAKE MEANING

• **Thought-Provoking Activities to Generate New Ideas** Following each selection, you'll have the chance to explore your own ideas and learn more about what you read.

Explore Your Reading takes you into, through, and beyond the actual selection to help you investigate the writing and its ideas more closely.

Develop Reading and Literary Skills expands your knowledge of literary forms, terms, and techniques. Following up on the Read Actively activities and strategies, you will learn more about how writing communicates.

Ideas for Writing and **Ideas for Projects** offer you the chance to create your own answers to your own questions. How does the selection relate to you? Where can you learn more? What cross-curricular connections can you make? These ideas features help you try things out yourself.

Enjoy this book!

All the features of this program fit together to develop your interest, skills, and, ultimately, your ability to learn.

Have fun with the time you spend with this book. Look at the art, plan for unit level projects, look for connections between selections. Pay attention to your own questions—finding the answers to those may be the most rewarding of all.

Joining Hands

Illustration Jim Osborn, Courtesy of the artist

"Here's my hand …"
"And mine, with my heart in it."

—Shakespeare—*The Tempest*

Get the Picture

Think about the quotation from William Shakespeare as you look at the picture of the hands reaching toward one another. Clearly, offering your hand is a sign of caring—of relationships.

As you read through this unit about Joining Hands, you might ask yourself questions, like the following, about relationships:

• How Do We Care for One Another?
• What Are Friends For?
• How Are We Different but Really the Same?

These questions, as well as others you may think of, will help you explore the relationships that enrich your world—and the world of literature. Keep a journal as you read this unit. Jot down thoughts you have about these questions, ideas sparked by the selections, and reflections you have on what you've read.

Activities
In a Group Discuss ways people "join hands" to achieve a common goal. Choose one of the situations and improvise a two-minute skit. Then discuss the actions and reactions of each of the "characters."

Activities
On Your Own Make a bookmark that expresses how you join hands with authors and characters through reading. Write a quotation or catchy phrase on your bookmark and decorate it with original artwork.

Project Preview ....

You can also respond to questions about joining hands by working on projects. Preview the following projects and think about which one you might do. For more details, see pages B128–B129.

- **Multimedia Presentation on Customs and Relationships**
- **Mural**
- **Interaction Skits**
- **Authors and Characters Talk Show**
- **Game for Younger Children**

Read Actively

How does my reading relate to my world?

How can I get more from what I read?

The answer to questions like these is to be an active reader, an *involved* reader. As an active reader, you are in charge of the reading situation!

The following strategies tell how to think as an active reader. You don't need to use all of these strategies all of the time. Feel free to choose the ones that work best in each reading situation.

BEFORE YOU READ

PREVIEW

What do the title and the pictures suggest? What will the selection say about "Joining Hands"?

GIVE YOURSELF A PURPOSE

What is the author communicating? What will you learn about the theme? How will the selection relate to your life?

REACH INTO YOUR BACKGROUND

What do you know already?

WHILE YOU READ

AFTER YOU READ

PREDICT

What do you think will happen? Why? You can change your mind as you read along.

ASK QUESTIONS

What's happening? Why do the characters do what they do? Why does the author give you certain details or use a particular word? Your questions help you gather evidence and make inferences.

VISUALIZE

What would these events and characters look like in a movie? How would the writer's descriptions look in a photograph?

CONNECT

Are characters like you or someone you know? What would you do in a similar situation?

RESPOND

Talk about what you've read. What did you think?

ASSESS YOURSELF

How did you do? Were your predictions on target? Did you find answers to your questions?

FOLLOW UP

Show what you know. Get involved. Do a project. Keep learning.

The model that begins on the next page shows Wanda Todd's thoughts while actively reading "Friends All of Us."

My name is Wanda Todd. I'm a student at Hampton Middle School in Detroit, Michigan. I enjoyed this true story about a special memory. The notes you see in the margins of the selection show my thoughts and questions as I read this selection.

Wanda Todd

The name of this story seems to say the writer is going to tell us to be kind to one another. [Preview]

Friends All of Us
Pablo Neruda

Chile—that's in South America. [Background]

One time, investigating in the backyard of our house in Temuco [Chile] the tiny objects and minuscule beings of my world, I came upon a hole in one of the boards of the fence. I looked through the hole and saw a landscape like that behind our house, uncared for, and wild. I moved back a few steps, because I sensed vaguely that something was about to happen. All of a sudden a hand appeared—a tiny hand of a boy about my own age. By the time I came close again, the hand was gone, and in its place there was a marvelous white sheep.

The sheep's wool was faded. Its wheels had escaped. All of this only made it more authentic. I had never seen such a wonderful sheep. I looked back through the hole but the boy had disappeared. I went into the house and brought out a treasure of my own: a pinecone, opened, full of odor and resin,[1] which I adored. I set it down in the same spot and went off with the sheep.

Why doesn't he just go inside? [Question]

I never saw either the hand or the boy again. And I have never again seen a sheep like that either. The toy I lost finally in a fire. But even now, in 1954, almost 50 years old, whenever I pass a toy shop, I look furtively into the window, but it's no use. They don't make sheep like that any more.

I can understand what he's saying about how important it is to have people that care about you. [Connect]

I have been a lucky man. To feel the intimacy of brothers is a marvelous thing in life. To feel the love of people whom we love is a fire that feeds our life. But to feel the affection that comes from those whom we do not know, from those unknown to us, who are watching over our sleep and solitude, over our dangers and our weaknesses—that is something still greater and more beautiful because it widens out the boundaries of our being, and unites all living things.

---

1. **resin** (REZ in) *n.*: A sticky substance, like sap, that oozes from some plants and trees.

That exchange brought home to me for the first time a precious idea: that all of humanity is somehow together. That experience came to me again much later; this time it stood out strikingly against a background of trouble and persecution

It won't surprise you then that I attempted to give something resiny, earthlike, and fragrant in exchange for human brotherhood. Just as I once left the pinecone by the fence, I have since left my words on the door of so many people who were unknown to me, people in prison, or hunted, or alone.

That is the great lesson I learned in my childhood, in the backyard of a lonely house. Maybe it was nothing but a game two boys played who didn't know each other and wanted to pass to the other some good things of life. Yet maybe this small and mysterious exchange of gifts remained inside me also, deep and indestructible, giving my poetry light.

Does the boy grow up to be an author? [Question]

Yes—the boy did grow up to be a writer—a poet. [Answer questions]

I wonder if he ever wrote a poem about his experience. I'll try to find out more about this writer's work. [Follow up]

Long before **Pablo Neruda** (1904–1973) won the Nobel Prize for literature in 1971, he was known and beloved by people around the world as a Spanish-speaking poet as well as a political figure from his native country of Chile, in South America.

Words to Know

minuscule (MI nuhs kyool) *adj.*: Very small; tiny
vaguely (VAYG lee) *adv.*: In a hazy, uncertain way
authentic (aw THEN tik) *adj.*: Real and believable
furtively (FER tiv lee) *adv.*: In a hidden way
intimacy (IN tuh muh see) *n.*: A very personal closeness
solitude (SAHL uh tood) *n.*: The condition of being alone
persecution (per suh KYOO shuhn) *n.*: Cruel and unfair treatment, often because of politics, religion, or race

Respond

- Why do you think Neruda remembers this childhood incident so clearly?
- Sketch or jot down notes describing what you would have given in return for the sheep.

Activities
MAKE MEANING

Explore Your Reading
Look Back (Recall)

1. When and where does this incident take place?
2. What gifts do the boys give each other?

Think It Over (Interpret)

3. How is the pinecone like Neruda's writing?
4. How does the exchange of gifts give "light" to the poetry of Pablo Neruda?
5. Why does this memory still have an effect on Neruda's life?

Go Beyond (Apply)

6. How can a story about two people be meaningful to many people?

Develop Reading and Literary Skills
Recognize Layers of Meaning

As you read this incident from Neruda's life, you probably realized that the tale is not as simple as it seems. On one level, it is just a story of two boys exchanging simple gifts. On another level, it taught Neruda something about his life. On yet a third level, it holds a message for all people. Copy the graphic organizer into your notebook. In the circles, write down your ideas about "Friends All of Us."

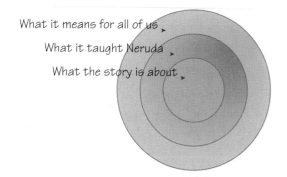

What it means for all of us

What it taught Neruda

What the story is about

1. What is this true story about?
2. What did Neruda learn from the experience?
3. What is the message of Neruda's story?

Ideas for Writing

In this story from his life, Neruda expresses the gratitude he feels for a simple gift given to him by a stranger—a gift that in some ways inspired Neruda to share his gift of writing with the world.

Letter Most of the gifts you get probably come from people you know. Write a letter of thanks to someone who has given you an especially meaningful gift.

Gift Poem What gift can you share with the world? Write a poem about it. Focus on descriptions and images that show what the gift is and why you want to share it.

Ideas for Projects

Interview Think of someone in your school or community who gives others the gift of his or her time and talents. Prepare some questions to ask that person in an interview. Either take notes or, if possible, tape-record or videotape the responses. Share the completed interview in a written or recorded form with your classmates.

Mobile Make a mobile to show the importance of sharing with others. Draw or cut out magazine pictures that convey the idea of sharing. Paste the pictures onto cardboard shapes. Put a picture on each side, since your mobile will be seen from all sides. Then string the pictures in groups and hang them from a stick or coat hanger. Display the finished mobiles from your classroom ceiling.

How Am I Doing?

Take a moment to answer these questions:
Which active reading strategy helped me the most?

Which layer of meaning was most significant to me?

How Do We Care for One Another?

Student Art *Family Photos* Hila Sela
Memorial Jr./Sr. High School, Fair Lawn, New Jersey

from I Saved a Winter Just for You

Student Writing Katie Kramer
Santa Fe Preparatory School, Santa Fe, New Mexico

When I was a little girl
Climbing stairs and chasing calico cats,
There was a cedar chest,
And I would go treasure hunting.
There were scrapbooks and letters and birthday cards.
There were old pictures of young couples
With soft skin and frozen faces.
There was a love letter from the cowboy
That mother married. It was funny.
I found the secret of life when I was six years old.

How do traditions get started?

Reach Into Your Background

Most cultural groups have traditions—shared customs, stories, and beliefs passed down from one generation to the next. Traditions enrich our lives by tying the past to the present and the future. For instance, when we celebrate the Fourth of July with fireworks, we are sharing the experience with all the generations before who celebrated the holiday with fireworks. It's a tradition. The following activities will help you and your classmates identify some of the traditions that enrich your lives:

- Brainstorm for a list of traditions that class members know from their own experience or from reading.
- Take turns sharing what you know about the origins, purposes, and activities of the different traditions.

Sharing America, 1990 (detail of quilt)
Little Stitch Makers, LaCrosse, Wisconsin
Museum of American Folk Art

Read Actively

Visualize Characters

Traditions enrich your life by giving you a connection with people from the past. You can almost see them carrying out the tradition in much the same way as you do. **Visualizing** them in this way, creating mental pictures, helps you understand them. In the same way, you can enrich your reading by visualizing **characters**—the people in the stories. Visualizing characters helps you connect with them and understand them.

As you read "The Haste-Me-Well Quilt," make quick sketches or jot down details about how you visualize the characters.

The Haste-Me-Well Quilt
Elizabeth Yates

Simon lay very still in his bed. Outside, birds were singing in the apple tree; cows were mooing by the pasture bars as they did when it was time to be milked.

Sometimes the wind flapped a little at the drawn shade, lifting it and letting in a flash of sunshine to frolic through the darkened room. But Simon only turned restlessly on the bed, kicking at the sheet and sending his books and toys onto the floor. He was tired of lying still, tired of being sick. He was cross at the world.

📖 **Read Actively**

Visualize this scene.

A set of crayons that his father had brought him that morning toppled off the bed. The blue one lay broken. Simon was glad it was broken and wished they all were. He did not want to use them. He hated crayons. He hated everyone. He—

Then the door opened slowly. It was Grandmother, with something over her arm. She went quietly across to the window, raising the shade so the sunlight could come into the room. The scent of lilacs came, too, and the song of birds.

Simon screwed up his eyes and said crossly, "Don't want any light, want darkness."

Grandmother laid the quilt she was carrying across the end of his bed; then she sat down on the bed and took one of Simon's hands in hers. She put her other hand on his forehead. Her touch was cool and gentle, like the water of a brook on a summer day. Simon opened his eyes and stared at her.

Words to Know

frolic (FRAHL ik) v.: Play or romp about

America Discovered Through Quilts: Past, Present and Future, 1990
Jean A. Natrop, Museum of American Folk Art

"'Truly the light is sweet, and a pleasant thing it is for the eyes to behold the sun,'" Grandmother said slowly. "That's in the Bible, Simon. Grandfather read it to me this morning before he went out to plant the corn."

Simon opened his eyes wider. Grandmother had put something at the end of his bed. It was a patchwork quilt. Simon looked at it curiously. It was made not of odd-shaped patterns sewn together, but of tiny pictures of real things.

"Granny, what have you got?" he asked, forgetting how cross he was at the world, forgetting his hot, heavy head.

"This, Simon, is a quilt that we have always laid on the bed of sickness. Because of that it is called the Haste-Me-Well Quilt."

Deftly she shook it out of its folds and spread it over Simon, saying as she did so, "Grandfather needs you to help him on the farm. Your father wants to take a strong boy back to the city with him. It's time that you got well."

"Is it a magic quilt?" Simon asked, fingering it warily.

📖 **Read Actively**

Predict how the quilt will help Simon.

Grandmother nodded. "Perhaps, but a very special kind of magic."

Then something happened to Simon. He smiled. And because he had not smiled for a week but only thought how sorry he was for himself, his lips were a little stiff at the corners. But the smile lived on in his eyes, dark and deep, almost as dark as his thick black hair.

Discover America One Patch at a Time, 1990
Joyce Winterton Stewart, Rexburg, Idaho, Museum of American Folk Art

"Tell me about it, please," he said, snuggling down under the quilt and pulling Grandmother's hand up to his chin.

"Long ago, Simon," she began, "more than a hundred years ago, my grandmother—"

"*Your* grandmother!" he exclaimed—such a long way that seemed to reach back into the past.

"Yes," Grandmother nodded, "Lucy, her name was, made the quilt. She lived on a farm on the moors[1] close to the Scottish border. She was not much older than you when she started it, and she finished it when she was seventeen—in time for her marriage. All of her friends were making quilts, but they made them out of bits and pieces of calico cut into squares or circles or triangles and sewed together into pretty patterns. Lucy was gay and strong, with quick fingers and a lively mind. She wanted to do something different, so she cut out her bits of calico into little pictures."

Grandmother bent over the quilt, and Simon propped his head up to follow her finger's journey across it.

"See, here is the farmhouse where she lived on the edge of the moors. Here are the chickens and the old tabby. Here is the postman, the muffin man with his bell, and the peddler who came with trinkets and ribbons and pots and pans. Here is her father, going off with his crook for the sheep. Here is a teakettle and the footstool at her feet, tables and fire tongs, watering cans and a bellows, horses and snails, a great castle, and a coach with dashing horses. Things she read about in books are here, like dragons and kangaroos and gladiators,[2] as well as the

---

1. moors (MŌŌRZ) *n.*: Wide open fields of marshy land.

2. gladiators (GLAD ee ay terz) *n.*: In ancient Rome, the men who fought against other men or against wild animals for the entertainment of the crowds.

latest fashion in bonnets and a mirror to try them on before"— Grandmother got more and more excited as her fingers flew across the quilt and she pointed out its wonders.

"It *is* a magic quilt," Simon agreed.

"Whatever young Lucy saw as interesting, useful, or amusing," Grandmother went on, "she snipped out of calico and sewed onto a white square, which was sewed to all the other white squares. Then, see, Simon, around the border she planted an old-fashioned garden!"

"It's like your garden, Granny, here at Easterly Farm!" Simon exclaimed.

"That's because it was *her* garden," Grandmother said quietly.

"It was?"

"Yes. When Lucy married, she and her husband came to America, here to this New England countryside. It was close to wilderness then, you must remember, but with their own hands they built this house; and while Silas cleared the fields and planted his crops and raised his stock, Lucy brought up her family—five boys and five girls, each one with a name from the Bible."

"And the quilt?"

"It must have meant everything to her in those days, for it was all her past—beautiful and orderly and gracious—and she brought it forward into a life of hardship and toil and privation.[3] To her it was the tale of an age that was gone forever, costumes and customs, the little things used in a house and the larger things that though never seen were talked about; and she made it the background of a new life."

"How did it get its name, Granny? You haven't told me that."

Grandmother smiled. "The quilt used to lie on the guest bed, for all to admire it and for its occasional use. Then one day Peter

---

3. **toil and privation:** Hard work and sacrifice.

Friends Sharing America, 1990
Three Friends, Clinton, Michigan, Museum of American Folk Art

was sick. He was the eldest of the five boys. He was wracked with chills and nothing they could do seemed to warm him. Lucy put all the blankets she had over him, and finally the quilt. Soon, oh, much sooner than anyone thought possible, the chills shivered themselves away and he went to sleep. Ever after that the quilt was put on the bed of a child who was sick."

"Was it ever on my father's bed?" Simon asked.

"Yes." Grandmother looked away. "Once when he fell from the barn during the haying and hurt his back, the doctor said that he could not do anything for him because he could not keep him still long enough." Grandmother smiled and turned back to look at

Words to Know

deftly (DEFT lee) *adv.*: Skillfully and easily
warily (WAYR uh lee) *adv.*: Carefully and cautiously
peddler (PED ler) *n.*: A person who walked from town to town selling things
wracked (RAKT) *adj.*: Overcome with great suffering

Memories Playground, 1988 Sheila Ruth Mahoney
Zephyr, Ontario, Canada, Museum of American Folk Art

Simon. "Grandfather and I didn't give up so easily. We put the quilt on his bed and for days and days afterward your father had wonderful adventures with it. He was always going to tell me about them, but he always forgot to."

Simon was looking drowsy, so Grandmother smoothed the folds of the quilt as it lay over him and stole softly from the room.

Simon moved his fingers lovingly over the quilt. He stroked the furry rabbit and called to the horse galloping across the field. He waved to the coach as it dashed along the road to London, and he bought a muffin from the muffin man. Then he opened the

Words to Know

confided (cahn FĪ did) *v.*: Shared a private thought or idea

incredulous (in KREJ yoo luhs) *adj.*: Unwilling or unable to believe

gate in the white fence that enclosed the farmhouse from the rolling moors and went up to the wide front door. Seeing it from a distance, he had not thought he could possibly go through the door, but the nearer he got to it the more of a size they were, and he found himself going into the house.

Inside, it was cool and quiet. His steps echoed a bit on the polished brick of the floor, but the sound did not disturb the tabby sleeping by the hearth. On the hob[4] hung a fat kettle with a wisp of steam coming from its spout, saying as clearly as any words that whoever might be passing would be welcome to a dish of tea.

Simon went to the end of a passage and pushed open another door. A young girl was sitting by an open window. Grandmother had not told him what Lucy looked like, but Simon knew right away that this was Lucy. The quilt lay in a heap on the floor beside her; on a table nearby were scissors and thread, and bits and pieces of cloth. Simon crossed the room and stood beside Lucy. She looked up at him.

📖 **Read Actively**

Ask yourself how it is possible for Simon to have this conversation with his great-grandmother.

"I have a little boy in the quilt," she said. "There's no room for you."

"That's all right," Simon replied, "but mayn't I sit down and watch you?"

"If you wish," she smiled, "but it's all finished."

Simon sat down, tailor fashion before her, cupping his chin in his hands.

"Two hundred and seventy-four squares around a center panel, bordered by flowers," Lucy went on. "It's all done, but it's well it is for I'm going away next week."

"Where are you going?" Simon asked.

"To the New World." Lucy looked out of the window and Simon thought her voice

---

4. hob (HAHB) *n.*: A little ledge at the back of the fireplace for keeping a kettle or saucepan warm.

throbbed, like a bird's on a low note. "I shall never see England again, never the rolling moors, nor the mountains of Scotland."

"*Never?*" Simon echoed. What a long time that was.

She shook her head slowly. "Ever since I was a little girl I have been cutting out and patching together the things that are my world. Now I can take my old world with me into the new. Once I wished I could draw pictures, go to London, and study to be an artist, but—"

"Why didn't you?" Simon demanded.

"If I had been a man I should have, but a girl doesn't do those things. Scissors, thread, thimble, calico—those are my artist's tools. Fingers are wonderful things, aren't they, little boy? You put a tool in them—it doesn't matter what it is—a hoe, a churn, a needle, a spoon—and they do the rest."

"My father gave me crayons to draw with," Simon confided. "I want to be an artist someday."

"Crayons?" Lucy looked as if the word were strange to her. "They'll not make you an artist, but fingers will."

"Why?"

"Because they are friends to all you're feeling. I didn't know when I started this quilt that it would mean so much to me. Now, though I'm going far away, everything I love is going with me."

Simon stroked the quilt. "It will be nice to have it on your bed, won't it?"

She laughed. "Oh, it won't ever be on my bed. It's too good for that! It'll be in the spare room, for guests to use when they come to stay with us."

"And it will be on the children's beds whenever they are sick," Simon went on.

Lucy looked at him, amazed. "What a strange idea!"

The Land of Counterpane
ROBERT LOUIS STEVENSON

When I was sick and lay a-bed,
I had two pillows at my head,
And all my toys beside me lay
To keep me happy all the day.

5 And sometimes for an hour or so
I watched my leaden soldiers go,
With different uniforms and drills,
Among the bed-clothes, through the hills;

And sometimes sent my ships in fleets
10 All up and down among the sheets;
Or brought my trees and houses out,
And planted cities all about.

I was the giant great and still
That sits upon the pillow-hill,
15 And sees before him, dale and plain,
The pleasant land of counterpane.

"It will make them well."

"Do you really think so, little boy?" Lucy looked incredulous, then her eyes gazed far away as if she did not see Simon at all and she said slowly, "The quilt could never do that, but perhaps the thoughts I have sewed into it could." Her eyes came back from the faraway place and she looked closely at Simon. "What is your name, little boy? I would like to know in case we meet again."

"Simon."

She wrinkled her brows. "Yes, Simon. For a moment I thought you were one of my boys." She went on looking at him as if wondering why he seemed so familiar, then she shook her head.

"There's magic in the quilt," Simon commented, reaching out and touching it.

"Magic? What strange words you use."

"But there is," Simon insisted. "How did you put it in?"

She laughed gaily. "What you call magic is just being happy in what you are doing, loving it the way you love the morning or the new lambs every spring. There's strength in happiness."

The blind was flapping at the window. The scent of lilacs filled the air. The sun, dropping low over the hills, was coming into the room like an arrow of gold. Simon drew his hands over the quilt and propped himself up on his elbows. On the floor lay his crayons, one of them broken.

He slipped out of bed and gathered the crayons together into their box, then he pushed the pillows up straight and climbed back into bed. Leaning against the pillows, he curved his knees up so his drawing pad might rest against them. He was sad that the blue crayon was broken, for so much blue was needed to arch the sky over the rolling moors and give life to Lucy's eyes. But he would manage somehow.

Quickly he worked, his fingers strong and free, eager with happiness, hurrying to do something for Grandmother that he might have a present for her when she came back to his room.

The door pushed open a little, then wider as Grandmother saw Simon. On the table by his bed she laid a small tray.

"There's a glass of milk from the afternoon's milking, Simon," she said. "Grandfather sent it up to you, and I thought you'd like a molasses cookie from a batch I've just made."

Simon finished his picture quickly.

"See, Granny, I have a present for you!"

Grandmother smiled as she took the drawing. It was a happy picture; well-done, too. Simon's father would be pleased with it. A young girl and a patchwork quilt, and in the background a small stone farmhouse. Grandmother looked closer. It was the Haste-Me-Well Quilt and Lucy looking at the world with eyes of wonder.

"Thank you, Simon, thank you very much, but I did not tell you my grandmother's eyes were blue, did I?"

Simon shook his head. "Were they?"

"Yes, blue as morning light on the mountains, and her fingers were fine and strong."

Fingers were wonderful things, Simon thought. It didn't much matter what they held if they held it with joy. Simon looked dreamily across the room. He was trying to remember something to tell Grandmother, but whatever it was it was slipping from him like a rainbow before full sunshine.

"May I get up now, Granny, please?" he asked.

A surprised smile lighted Grandmother's face. She nodded and began to fold up the Haste-Me-Well Quilt.

Respond

- Which one of the characters would you like to have in your family? Explain.
- Tell a partner which character seemed most real to you and why.

How does Newbery Medal-winner Elizabeth Yates explain her desire to write stories? In an interview about her childhood she said: "I could think up stories about the houses I passed, or perhaps just about [my horse] Bluemouse and me as we journeyed through the day and the country together; and everything had a story." About her goals in life, she has said: "I want to put myself on the side of good, no matter how small my service, and so make my life count in the sum total."

Activities
MAKE MEANING

 ## Explore Your Reading
Look Back (Recall)

1. Who is Lucy?

Think It Over (Interpret)

2. Why is Simon so disagreeable at the beginning of the story?
3. How does the quilt change Simon's attitude?
4. How does Simon's grandmother help Simon to feel better?

Go Beyond (Apply)

5. Based on Lucy's and Simon's experiences, explain how beginning and continuing traditions can be helpful to people in difficult times.

 ## Develop Reading and Literary Skills
Examine Character Traits

The quilt helped Simon visualize, or form a mental picture of, Lucy's farm in Scotland. Similarly, the details you jotted down or sketched as you read helped you visualize the characters. You may have pictured Lucy's lively blue eyes or Grandmother's gentle smile. As you got to know the people in the story you could study their **character traits,** qualities that made up their personalities. Review your notes and pictures to find details that made the characters come alive for you. You might even want to review the story to find other details that reveal character traits.

1. List one detail for each character that helped you form a mental picture of him or her.
2. Choose one of the characters and describe his or her personality in your own words.
3. How did your image of Simon change from the beginning to the end of the story? Explain.
4. Explain how visualizing the characters helped you to understand their personalities.

Ideas for Writing

As Simon discovers, finding out about an old tradition can lead to new and interesting experiences.

Magazine Article Write a magazine article that explains how a particular tradition began. The article can be about a personal family tradition or a tradition of a cultural group. Get started by talking to older family members or consulting library resources.

Short Story Write a short story that tells how a character learns about a family tradition or a tradition related to his or her cultural heritage. You can use a real tradition from your family or make up a tradition that seems believable.

Ideas for Projects

Story Advertisement Create an advertisement for "The Haste-Me-Well Quilt." Combine a picture that shows something about the story with a title or caption about the relationships and traditions the story tells about.

Quilt of Traditions Work with a group to create a quilt about traditions people share. Have each group member create a "quilt square" representing a tradition. Use construction paper, magazine pictures, photos, felt, and other available materials to create the squares. Assemble the squares to make the complete quilt and display it in the classroom.

How Am I Doing?

Respond to these questions in your journal:
Which character was I able to visualize most clearly? What helped me to visualize the character?
How can visualizing help me read other forms of literature?

What is our responsibility to one another?

Reach Into Your Background

You've probably wished a friend or family member could know what it's like to be you, but did you ever try to understand what it's like to be someone else? You can learn a lot by putting yourself in *someone else's* shoes. The following activities can help you and a partner or group "wear someone else's shoes":

- Brainstorm for situations in which two people might disagree. Role-play how the situations can be resolved.
- Choose to be story characters who are actually very different from you. Take turns asking "yes-no" questions trying to discover each other's identities.

Read Actively
Identifying Problems

You've probably discovered that you can learn something about yourself by acting as someone else.

You can learn things about yourself by reading literature as well. Identifying the problems faced by characters helps you make sense of their actions throughout the story—and allows you to think about whether you would do the same *if you were in their shoes.*

As you read the story, identify the problems faced by the characters. Jot them down on a chart like the one shown.

Character	Problem
Father	
Mother	Wants the house to herself
Boy	
Grandfather	Lives in a cold room – alone

The Boy and His Grandfather
Rudolfo Anaya

In the old days it was not unusual to find several generations living together in one home. Usually, everyone lived in peace and harmony, but this situation caused problems for one man whose household included, besides his wife and small son, his elderly father.

It so happened that the daughter-in-law took a dislike to the old man. He was always in the way, she said, and she insisted he be removed to a small room apart from the house.

Because the old man was out of sight, he was often neglected. Sometimes he even went hungry. They took poor care of him, and in winter the old man often suffered from the cold. One day the little grandson visited his grandfather.

"My little one," the grandfather said, "go and find a blanket and cover me. It is cold and I am freezing."

The small boy ran to the barn to look for a blanket, and there he found a rug.

"Father, please cut this rug in half," he asked his father.

"Why? What are you going to do with it?"

"I'm going to take it to my grandfather because he is cold."

"Well, take the entire rug," replied his father.

"No," his son answered, "I cannot take it all. I want you to cut it in half so I can save the other half for you when you are as old as my grandfather. Then I will have it for you so you will not be cold."

His son's response was enough to make the man realize how poorly he had treated his own father. The man then brought his father back into his home and ordered that a warm room be prepared. From that time on he took care of his father's needs and visited him frequently every day.

Celestino Harley Brown, Courtesy of the artist

Words to Know

neglected (ni GLEKT id) *adj.*: Not cared for; ignored

frequently (FREE kwuhnt lee) *adv.*: Often; many times

El Muchacho y el Abuelito
José Griego y Maestas

Este era un hombre que no tenía más familia que su esposa y un hijito de cinco años. El hombre también tenía a su cargo a su padre anciano a quien lo asistían en la casa. Más como la nuera no quería a su suegro, mandó apartar al anciano, retirándolo de la casa donde vivían ellos. Allá le mandaban de comer algunos días y otros días no. En tiempos fríos no cuidaban de él y el pobre viejito sufría mucho. Un día se arrimó su nietecito a donde él estaba y le dijo el anciano:

"Hijito, búscame una garra por ahí para cobijarme. Me estoy helando de frío."

El muchachito fue corriendo a la despensa a buscar una garra y halló un pedazo de jerga. Le llevó el pedazo de jerga a su padre y le dice:

"Córteme esta jerga por la mitad."

"¿Para qué? ¿Qué vas a hacer con ese pedazo?"

"Voy a llevárselo a mi abuelito, porque tiene frío."

"Pues llévasela entera."

"No," le dijo, "no la llevo toda. Quiero que me la corte en la mitad porque quiero guardar el otro pedazo para cuando usted esté como mi abuelito. Entonces se la llevo a usted para que se cobije."

Aquella respuesta del muchachito fue suficiente para que el hombre reconociera la ingratitud que estaba haciendo con su padre. El hombre trujo a su padre anciano a su casa e hizo que le prepararan un cuarto y le dieran asistencia adecuada a sus necesidades. De ese tiempo en adelante él mismo cuidaba de su padre en la tarde y en la mañana.

 **Respond**

- If you could talk to one character in the story, who would it be? Why?
- Tell a partner what you would say to one of the characters in the story.

Rudolfo Anaya (1937–) has spent his life in New Mexico. He has written and published English versions of *Cuentos* (stories) about Mexican American people in the Southwest. As for himself, he says that in New Mexico, "everyone tells stories, it is a creative pastime. I was hooked early on the power of the word, in the relationships between the characters of the stories."

Explore Your Reading

Look Back (Recall)

1. Why does the grandfather live in a separate room?

Think It Over (Interpret)

2. What words would you use to describe the character of the grandfather? What details in the tale support your response?
3. Compare and contrast the characters of the boy and his father. Use details from the folk tale to illustrate your points.

Go Beyond (Apply)

4. In what ways could this folk tale apply to people who are not in the same family?

Developing Reading and Literary Skills

Apply Solutions to Problems in Folk Tales

Look over the chart you created while reading the folk tale. Although the characters are imaginary, their problems teach real lessons. For instance, this is a folk tale about a grandfather needing to get warm, but the lesson it teaches applies to many other situations. Often in folk tales, the characters face problems caused by common feelings such as fear and greed, and solved by virtues such as generosity and compassion.

By solving problems in folk tales you can learn lessons that you can apply to real-life situations. Refer to the notes on your chart as you answer the questions.

1. Name one problem faced by each of the characters.
2. What feelings or emotions contributed to the father's problem? Explain.
3. Whose problem does not seem to be solved at the end of the story? What solution would you suggest?
4. What is the lesson of this folk tale that you could apply to real-life situations?

Ideas for Writing

How can you use this folk tale's lessons about relationships?

Public Service Advertisement The problem faced by the family in "The Boy and His Grandfather" is one faced by many families—that is, how do members of different generations learn to get along with one another. Write a public service advertisement that gives suggestions about how older and younger people in a family can learn to communicate and respect one another. Include pictures, if desired, or videotape the advertisement if possible.

Folk Tale This folk tale teaches a lesson about the way people treat one another. Write a folk tale of your own—or retell one you've heard or read— that teaches a lesson about how to care for others.

Ideas for Projects

A World of Responsibility Poster How are people your age responsible to their families? Create a poster that uses pictures, graphs, or charts to show ways in which students contribute to family life in the United States or in other cultures you know about.

Thank-You Cards Create a greeting card for someone who has shown special care for you. Write a thank-you in the form of a poem or brief paragraph for the inside of the card. Illustrate the cover of the card with a symbol or image that represents caring— for example, joined hands.

How Am I Doing?

Take a moment to answer these questions:

Which character's problem helped me learn something about myself?

Which questions best helped me understand the folk tale?

Activities PREVIEW

Father William   by Lewis Carroll
The Little Boy and the Old Man   by Shel Silverstein

What makes a person old?

Reach Into Your Background

Sometimes it's hard to remember that older people were once young students like you. Someday, you too will be an older person. Do you have fixed ideas, or *stereotypes,* of what older people are like? Try either or both of the following activities to explore your feelings about what it's like to get older:

- Brainstorm for a list of pros and cons about getting older. Discuss your ideas with a partner or group.
- Make a sketch or jot down a quick description of someone you consider "elderly."

Read Actively
Make Inferences

Unlike your classmates, writers rarely tell you directly what they think about a topic. Instead, you **make inferences**—that is, you draw conclusions about their message from the details they give you. You "read between the lines" and think about how the characters are portrayed, what kind of language is used, and so forth.

As you read the two poems in this section, make inferences about each writer's feelings and opinions. Ask yourself the following questions as you read:

- What are the characters saying or doing?
- Does it seem as if the poet likes what the character is saying or doing?

Make a copy of the poems in your notebook. Jot down notes in the margin to answer these questions and others you may have.

Geoff Goslon, The Image Bank

Father William
Lewis Carroll

"You are old, Father William," the young man said,
    "And your hair has become very white;
And yet you incessantly stand on your head—
    Do you think, at your age, it is right?"

5 "In my youth," Father William replied to his son,
    "I feared it might injure the brain;
But, now that I'm perfectly sure I have none,
    Why, I do it again and again."

"You are old," said the youth, "as I mentioned before,
10   And have grown most uncommonly fat;
Yet you turned a back-somersault in at the door—
    Pray, what is the reason of that?"

"In my youth," said the sage, as he shook his gray locks,
    "I kept all my limbs very supple
15 By the use of this ointment—one shilling[1] the box—
    Allow me to sell you a couple?"

"You are old," said the youth, "and your jaws are too weak
    For anything tougher than suet;[2]
Yet you finished the goose, with the bones and the beak—
20   Pray, how did you manage to do it?"

"In my youth," said his father, "I took to the law,
    And argued each case with my wife;
And the muscular strength which it gave to my jaw
    Has lasted the rest of my life."

25 "You are old," said the youth, "one would hardly suppose
    That your eye was as steady as ever;
Yet you balanced an eel on the end of your nose—
    What made you so awfully clever?"

"I have answered three questions, and that is enough,"
30   Said his father; "don't give yourself airs![3]
Do you think I can listen all day to such stuff?
    Be off, or I'll kick you downstairs!"

Respond

What do you think is the most amazing thing Father William does? Why?

Words to Know

incessantly (in SES uhnt lee) *adv.*: Without stopping (line 3)

youth (YOOTH) *n.*: A young person (line 9)

sage (SAYJ) *n.*: A very wise person (line 13)

locks (LAHKS) *n.*: Hair (line 13)

supple (SUHP uhl) *adj.*: Able to bend and move easily (line 14)

---

1. shilling *n.*: A British coin, not used anymore. It was worth about 12 cents.
2. suet (SOO it) *n.*: The fatty part of meat.
3. give yourself airs: Act more important or intelligent than you are.

The Little Boy and the Old Man
Shel Silverstein

Said the little boy, "Sometimes I drop my spoon."
Said the little old man, "I do that too."
The little boy whispered, "I wet my pants."
"I do that too," laughed the little old man.
5 Said the little boy, "I often cry."
The old man nodded, "So do I."
"But worst of all," said the boy, "it seems
Grown-ups don't pay attention to me."
And he felt the warmth of a wrinkled old hand.
10 "I know what you mean," said the little old man.

Respond

How does this poem affect the way you think about people's ages?

Lewis Carroll
(1832–1898)

Q: What did Lewis Carroll's young friend (the real-life version of Alice from *Alice's Adventures in Wonderland*) say about this adult author?

A: "He seemed to have an endless store of these fantastical tales, which he made up as he told them, drawing busily on a large sheet of paper all the time."

Shel Silverstein
(1932–)

Q: What does the author say about his adult life?

A: "I want to go everywhere, look at and listen to everything. You can go crazy with some of the wonderful stuff there is in life."

Activities
MAKE MEANING

Explore Your Reading

Look Back (Recall)

1. What actions do the little boy and the old man have in common in "The Little Boy and the Old Man"?

Think It Over (Interpret)

2. Why is the young man surprised at the actions of Father William?
3. Do you think of each of these poems as funny or serious? Why?
4. How would you describe the personality of the older man in each poem? What details in the poems support your ideas?

Go Beyond (Apply)

5. Why do you think each of these poems is included in the section "How Do We Care for One Another?"

Develop Reading and Literary Skills

Make Inferences About Theme

Both of these poems were written as conversations between an old man and a young one. Poetry is a kind of conversation—the poet speaks to you through the poem. As you read these two poems, you jotted down notes about what you thought the poet was saying to you. Based on what was said, and how it was said, you made **inferences**; you drew logical conclusions about each poet's message—the **theme** of the poem.

1. List two clues you noted in each poem that indicated the thoughts and feelings of the poet.
2. State the theme of each poem. Explain your statement with details you noted in the poems.

Ideas for Writing

These poems are now a part of your own thinking on age and youth.

Character Comparisons In a short composition, compare and contrast the personalities and interests of an older and younger person. They can be people you know or characters from literature.

Song Lyrics Write a song or a poem about an elderly person you admire. Publish the lyrics with an original drawing, a collage, or a photograph you think connects with the subject or mood of your song.

Ideas for Projects

Readers Theater Perform the dialogue in either "Father William" or "The Little Boy and the Old Man" with a partner. Record your performance on videotape or audiotape and play the recording for your classmates.

Young and Old Posters Lewis Carroll lived to be sixty-six years old and Shel Silverstein, still alive, was once a student your age. Research more biographical information about each of these popular authors. Create a "Young and Old" biography poster for them that shows what they were like as children and what they are (or were) like as adults. If you can, include a picture or photograph of each writer.

How Am I Doing?

Think about what you've learned by answering the following questions:

Which poem's theme was clearer to me? Why?

What did I do or make that shows how these poems affected the way I think about age?

What's important to you?

Reach Into Your Background

If you had to go on a long journey—alone—and never return to your home—what would you take with you? What if you could only take three things? What would be hardest to leave behind? Questions like these can help you think about what's important in your life. The following activities can help you explore your answers:

• Make a list of ten things that are important to you. Next to each item, write a number that ranks its importance.

• Discuss with a partner what things you would take and why.

Read Actively
Identify Symbols

Some of the things you chose for your "journey" probably stand for feelings, people, or memories. These choices are **symbols**, things that represent something else.

When you think of a bald eagle, you might think of it as a symbol of the United States, strength, freedom, history. It can stand for one or all of those ideas. That's the beauty of a symbol. There isn't just one "correct" meaning.

This story tells about the life and background of a young girl named Rosa from the mountains of Guatemala in Central America. There, the *quetzal* bird is a symbol for the Mayan people. It also stands for other ideas.

As you read the story, jot down your own ideas about the quetzal and other symbols you encounter in the story.

Skybird to the High Heavens

NANCY WHITE CARLSTROM

My name is Rosa. Rosa Lucas Paíz. I once lived in a land where footbridges dangled high above rushing streams and mountains stretched up green to the sky. Somehow the cows kept from falling off the steep cliffs.

"Grandmother, who keeps the cows in place?" I asked when I was a young girl.

"The same one who keeps the sun in the sky," my grandmother answered as she sat weaving on the floor of our house.

Corn grew in my land. Corn grew in patches on the side of the mountains where the cows did not fall. Grandmother said corn was one of the most important things we had. Corn gave us life.

My grandmother taught me how to weave. She had pieces of old weavings her grandmother gave to her when she was a girl. One day, she took them out and showed me.

"Rosa, these are the designs of our people." And she explained to me how each village used certain colors and designs in the weaving of cloth.

"I have saved these samples for many years, so I could pass them on to you. When I die, you will have them to use as patterns, so our own special weaving will live on."

As Grandmother taught me to weave, she told me stories about our land and its living things.

"Grandmother, tell me again about the time you saw the quetzal."[1]

And Grandmother told me yet another time about when she was a girl and traveled far to the lowlands with her family. There, as they passed through the jungle, Grandmother had glimpsed the most beautiful bird in the world. The quetzal had blue-green tail feathers that stretched out three feet long. On its head was a tuft of gold and its chest wore a blood-red vest.

"If only I could see a quetzal someday, Grandmother."

"Maybe you will, my child. Maybe you will."

That night, I dreamed I rode on the back of a quetzal. I felt the rush of the wind as we soared to the high heavens. In the morning, I told my grandmother about my dream.

"How could I ride a quetzal, Grandmother?" I asked. "Did the bird become large, or did I become small?"

"Perhaps the dream was telling you that soon you must become small and hide from the danger wandering through our land. No matter what happens, may you always remember the sweet smell of the earth, my child."

---

1. quetzal (ket SAHL)

Las Companeras De Chichicastenango 1992 Donna Clair, Courtesy of the artist

I knew my grandmother was talking about the war that was tearing our country apart, like a hideous beast. But still, I did not fully understand her warning.

And so, all morning as I did my chores, I daydreamed about becoming small. Small enough to hide behind the clay cooking pots my mother kept by the fire. Maybe if I jumped out I could surprise her and make her laugh.

I could be small enough to hide in an ear of corn and watch the sun glow on my father's back as he lifted the hoe.

"Father, why do you spend so many hours weeding the corn?" I asked, when he came home with rough hands and a tired back.

"Why, Rosa, if I allow the weeds to grow, the souls of the corn plants will move to cleaner fields. Then what would we eat, my daughter? How could we trade to buy the tools we need, the sandals you wear on your feet?"

"Sell the stories Grandmother tells as she weaves on her loom," I said with a laugh.

Father just shook his head, but Grandmother smiled to herself and I knew she would tell me another tale later, when the crickets sang.

That night, Grandmother told me of the great earthquake that leveled our village before I was born. She told me how the houses folded like paper and how giant rocks were tossed from the mountains like pebbles. It was a sad, true story.

"We thought the sun would fall from the sky that time. But it didn't, Rosa," she said quietly.

"Grandmother, when you saw the quetzal in the jungle, did you want to catch him and bring him home?"

"No, Rosa, I knew the quetzal was a bird of freedom. A cage would kill him. There are other ways to enjoy his beauty."

That night, my dreams were troubled. I could not ride the quetzal to the high heavens. I could not hide behind my mother's cooking pots or in the corn of my father's field.

"Where will I go?" I cried. "Where will I go?"

Words to Know

hideous (HID ee uhs) *adj.*: Horrible; dreadfully frightening
leveled (LEV uhld) *v.*: Flattened; demolished

In the morning, soldiers came and burned our village. First, I hid. Then, as the whole sky turned black, I ran and ran. I could not look back.

My name is Rosa. Rosa Lucas Paíz. I now live in a place far from where the footbridges dangle above the rushing streams and the mountains stretch green into the sky.

"Grandmother," I whisper, "the cows have fallen off the cliff. The sun has dropped from the heavens and the corn rots."

I miss the corn that gave me life. I miss the pot of water my mother kept boiling all day on the fire. I miss the hoe of my father chopping in time with our people for hundreds of years. I miss the stories my grandmother told and the threads of color she wove on the loom.

"Grandmother," I whisper, "what if I forget the sweet smell of the earth? What if they put all the quetzals into cages?"

This morning, as I walk to the place where I work in the refugee[2] camp, I am surprised to hear someone call my name.

"Rosa." The voice is thin, like burnt paper, almost ready to crumble into little pieces.

"Rosa."

It comes to me across the miles that I have traveled while running in the cold night and burning day—fleeing through the cornfields, meeting up with others from distant villages, living pressed up close, finding shelter together from the winter rains. I see again a shared blanket, a cup of water and warm tortillas[3] passed around, and these are like sparks of light in the darkness of my memories.

---

2. refugee (ref yoo JEE) *n.*: A person who has run from his or her home or country to escape war.

3. tortillas (tor TEE yuhz) *n.*: Very thin, flat, round cakes made of corn meal or flour.

"Rosa, Rosa, is that you, dear?"

And there before me is a shriveled little woman dressed in the *traje*[4] of my village: María Magdalena Rivas, my grandmother's friend. Tears stream down my face.

Here is someone who knew my mother who kept the fire going, my father who lifted the hoe, my grandmother who told the tales and wove the cloth.

And now I sob at my loss, and in the arms of that old, familiar woman from my village, I take comfort.

She reaches deep under the belt that wraps around and around her frail body and takes out a small packet, a packet worn from the journey she has made.

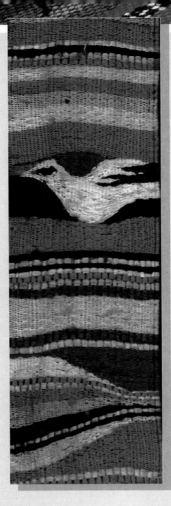

Inside are the sample pieces of weaving, the designs of our people. The pieces handed down by my great-great-grandmother. The ones my grandmother wanted me to have.

As I hold them in my hand, I see the brilliant colors, blue green, gold, and red—colors of the beautiful bird from the land I love. I know then that I will not forget. I will weave our patterns, designs of light, no matter where I live. I want the world to know and remember too.

"Grandmother," I whisper, "maybe it will keep the cows on the cliffs and the sun from falling. And just maybe tonight I will ride the quetzal, my skybird- to the high heavens."

---

4. **traje** (TRAH hay) *n.*: Traditional clothing.

Q: How did **Nancy White Carlstrom** become interested in writing for children ?

A: During high school, she worked in the children's department of a local library. She says,"That's where my dream of writing children's books was born."

Q: When and how did she write her first children's book?

A: Before the birth of her own children, Nancy Carlstrom owned and managed the Secret Garden children's book shop. Because of her involvement with literature for children, she learned about a special writing workshop conducted by an award-winning author. It was in this workshop that she completed her first published manuscript.

Q: What does she do today?

A: She lives and works as a writer in Fairbanks, Alaska. The landscape and the customs of the native people have become the subjects of her most recent books.

Respond

- Which of Rosa's experiences seem most real to you?
- Sketch or jot down a quick description of the most vivid impression you have of Rosa's home life.

Explore Your Reading

Look Back (Recall)

1. What is a quetzal?

Think It Over (Interpret)

2. What do you think the designs and colors in the weavings mean?
3. Why does Grandmother answer so many of Rosa's questions with stories?
4. How do Rosa's feelings about her life change in the story? Why?

Go Beyond (Apply)

5. What kinds of things do you think Rosa would pass along to future generations? What would they stand for?

Develop Reading and Literary Skills

Explain Symbols

As Rosa's grandmother explains, the quetzal is a bird that cannot be caged—to Rosa's grandmother it is a **symbol** of freedom and beauty. It stands for something besides itself. As you read the story, you came up with your own ideas about the quetzal and other symbols.

Copy and complete this cluster in your notebook. Add circles to show the symbols and what they meant to you and the characters.

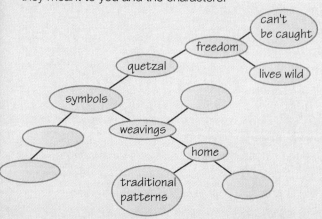

1. Name two symbols you identified and a main idea they stand for.
2. Explain at least two meanings for one of the symbols. Support your explanation with details from your chart.
3. What does the quetzal mean to you? Explain.

Ideas for Writing

Imagine that, just as Rosa is given the designs of her people, you are given the chance to choose something that tells about an important aspect in your life, family, or community.

Speech Write and deliver a speech about the item you would save as a symbol of something important to your life, your family, or your community. Include details that explain its meaning and why you think it should be preserved.

Journal Entry Write a journal entry in which you express the personal importance of this item to you.

Ideas for Projects

Interview Think of someone who knows a lot about the traditions you enjoy in your family or community, or someone who has a special skill you would like to learn. Prepare questions and interview that person. Present a written or recorded version of the interview for your class.

Mayan History Find out more about Mayan culture in Central America. Create a visual display that includes maps, artwork, and photos or magazine pictures. Put captions on the sections of your display. [Social Studies Link]

How Am I Doing?

Take a moment to answer these questions:

How did thinking about symbols help me understand this story?

How could the same strategy help me read other stories?

How Do We Care for One Another?

Think Critically About the Selections

The selections you have read in this section explore the question "How do we care for one another?" With a partner or small group, complete one or two of the following activities to show your understanding of the question. You can present your responses orally or in writing.

1. Several of the characters in this section learned lessons about family relationships. Which character's experiences made you look at your own family responsibilities in a new way? **(Synthesize)**

2. As you have seen in several of these selections, many families include people from very different age groups. Based on the selections you have read, what are some benefits of relationships between old and young people? **(Analyze; Draw Conclusions)**

3. Based on what you learned in one or more of these selections, how would you answer the question "How do we care for one another?" Support your answer with details from the selections. **(Form and Support a Generalization)**

Student Art **Family Photos** Hila Sela
Memorial Jr./Sr. High School, Fair Lawn, New Jersey

that will catch the attention of viewers and inform them that your poster communicates ideas about family relationships.

 Family Custom Different countries or cultures practice different customs within the family. Research family customs for a country or culture that interests you and use that information to create a booklet. Organize your information into sections with headings, such as "Sharing Meals," "Family Responsibilities," and others.

Projects

 Family Relationship Posters What did you learn about family relationships from reading the selections in this subunit? Express what you learned from the literature in a poster. Include pictures or photographs. Present words or phrases that communicate what you have learned. Come up with a title for your poster

 A Caring Song One idea that repeats in this subunit is that people care about one another. Write the lyrics to a song that expresses your feelings about caring for other people or the ideas communicated in one of the selections. You may include repeating lines and rhyming lines throughout your lyrics. Perform or record your finished song for your classmates.

Looking at Biography and

Barbara A. Lewis

Terms to know

Biography: The story of someone's life as told by a writer.

Autobiography: The story of a writer's own life.

What kinds of people are the subjects of biographies?

Most biographies are written about famous people. You might believe they were simply born to be great. Sometimes, though, ordinary people become great simply because they tried harder, refused to give up, walked two miles farther, or were brave for five minutes longer than anyone else. It's interesting to read about the achievements and personalities of other people.

How do I choose the subjects of my biographies?

My book *Kids With Courage* is a collection of biographies about ordinary kids like you, who have done extraordinary things. To find them, I contacted national groups who give awards to young people for their contributions. I found names in newspapers and magazines and from friends. I met many of the kids in person, but I interviewed most of them on the phone. I also talked with parents, teachers, friends, and anyone else who knew them well. Pages of notes and stacks of photographs piled up on my desk, along with enormous phone bills.

How do I bring my biographies to life?

Underlining my interview notes with different colors of markers helped me to organize their experiences and to unravel important events from those which were not. Then I could begin to re-weave these threads of experience into a plot or story of their lives.

What is an autobiography?

An autobiography is like a biography—except the writer tells his or her own life story. Like a biography, it covers the important events in the person's life. An added element of an autobiography is that it can include the writer's thoughts and feelings about the events—because he or she lived them!

What else do you write about in an autobiography?

You can write about less significant events as well. Vivid memories are an important part of an autobiography. In the autobiography "My Best Friend," Lessie Jones Little writes details of all the little things she and her friend talked about and did together. She tells how they would ". . . rake the cool, damp dirt on top of our feet and pack it down tight, then slide our feet out, leaving a little cave we called a frog house."

If you were writing your autobiography, you might write about the time you picked all the newly planted flowers in your neighbor's yard and gave them to your mother for her birthday. You might write about the time you took your pet snakes to school to show off

Literary Forms
Autobiography

and accidentally let them go loose. It's just as important to include the time you might have shared your lunch with a friend who had none.

What are the games you have played with your friends? What does your house look like? What do you think you look like? What makes you happy, sad, laugh, angry, teasing? What kinds of things do you hide in your closet, in your attic, under the back porch? How do you feel about your little brother and Aunt Margarita who always squeezes you too tightly and smells of pine soap and ravioli? These are the details you put in an autobiography.

Why read biographies and autobiographies?

Biographies and autobiographies, or life stories, are fun to read because they can make famous people seem like your friends. Once you know about a person's life, that person no longer seems so dusty and far away. Reading about people who are not so famous is fun too. It brings you in touch with the accomplishments of people like yourself. Reading biographies or autobiographies is a way of joining hands with others.

Barbara A. Lewis (1943–   ) writes for kids and about kids because she wants them to believe that you don't have to be famous, rich, or powerful to achieve great things. "*Anyone* can do courageous and wonderful things." She has four children of her own—Mike, Andrea, Christian, and Samuel.

If you'd like to read some of her biographies about kids, you will find them in her book *Kids With Courage.* Her work about students and their projects has also appeared in national magazines, newspapers, and on television.

Activities PREVIEW

Blintzes Stuffed With Cheese   by Kathleen Krull

How do you get to know someone?

Reach Into Your Background

Although we learn new things about the people in our lives all the time, we rarely think about how we do it! Think about someone you now know well whom you can actually remember meeting. What do you know about this person now? How did you get to know it?

Do one or both of these activities to explore the ways people get to know one another:

- In a small group, share experiences you've had that have helped you get to know someone.
- With a partner, prepare questions and conduct a mock interview with a famous person you would like to know well.

Illustration by Benjamin Levy

Read Actively

Explore Biographies

Usually, you get to know people by talking to them and sharing experiences with them. Reading a **biography,** the story of a person's life as told by someone else, allows you to learn about someone you might never meet in person.

Look ahead at the title and pictures that go with this biography of writer Isaac Bashevis Singer. What clues do they give you about Singer's personality? Copy the KWL chart into your notebook. In the first column, write what you already know about Singer from looking at the pictures. As you read, write new facts you learn about Singer in the third column. Write any questions you think of in the second column.

What I **K**now	What I **W**ant to Know	What I've **L**earned

Blintzes Stuffed With Cheese
Kathleen Krull

As a child in the Jewish ghetto of Warsaw, Poland, Icek-Herz Zynger studied the Jewish religion all day long at *cheder*[1] (elementary school). His family was so poor—at times starving—that sometimes his only toy was a dried palm branch, and he would play with it for days. Reading outside of school made him forget his physical discomforts, especially after he discovered the tales of Edgar Allan Poe.

But the rise of anti-Jewish feeling in Europe sometimes gave him thoughts of suicide. At age thirty-one, by then known as Isaac Bashevis Singer (Bashevis is a variation on his mother's name, Bathsheba), he came to the United States. His first wife, Runya, and their son, Israel, moved to Russia and eventually to Palestine. They all escaped the Holocaust,[2] when most Polish Jews, including some of Singer's family and friends, were killed by Nazis during World War II. All the places Singer had known in Poland were destroyed in the war; the world of his childhood was gone.

Singer began to re-create that old world in stories. He wrote in Yiddish (a mixture of German, Russian, and Slavic, written in Hebrew letters from right to left). He typed on a rickety Yiddish-character typewriter and helped translators convert the stories into English. He wrote articles for *The Jewish Daily Forward*, a New York paper that also published installments of his stories. "I have to force myself *not* to write," he admitted.

Singer was devastated by the death of his adored older brother, Israel Joshua, a well-known writer. Yet his grief drove him to work harder, and his next book, *The Family Moskat*, was the one that brought fame.

Singer was married to his second wife, Alma, for fifty-one years. She worked for Saks Fifth Avenue department store and supported both of them until his writing started to bring in money. They divided their time between an apartment in Manhattan and a condominium in south Florida.

Singer got up every morning at eight o'clock, had cereal and a grapefruit or apple, and then sometimes went back to bed, where he wrote notes in inexpensive lined notebooks. In the afternoons he took long walks, sometimes to the *Forward* office to deliver stories or to a cafeteria to meet old friends (they called him Bashevis). He seldom watched TV or went to the movies and didn't own a phonograph[3] (so he never heard any of the recordings made of his stories).

He owned parakeets that flew free and sometimes landed on his bald head, and his neighbors knew him as someone who kept

---

3. **phonograph** (FOHN uh grahf) *n*.: Record player.

---

1. **cheder** (HAY der)
2. **Holocaust** (HAHL uh kahst): The Nazi's systematic destruction of more than six million European Jews before and during World War II.

Words to Know

variation (var ee AY shuhn) *n*.: A slightly different form
convert (cahn VERT) *v*.: Change
devastated (DEV uhs tayt id) *adj*.: Overwhelmed; destroyed
seldom (SEL duhm) *adv*.: Rarely

Illustration by Benjamin Levy

the pigeons well fed. He stopped eating meat out of his concern for animals. He wasn't a strict vegetarian, though; he ate eggs and did love blintzes stuffed with cheese.

Though he was still unknown at age forty, Singer eventually became famous and wealthy. But even then he lived simply; he was eating in a neighborhood drugstore when he learned he had won the Nobel Prize in literature. On the plane to receive his award, he read about himself in *People* magazine.

Pale and bald, Singer was the first to say he resembled an imp from one of his own stories. He wore dark suits, white shirts, and plain ties. He seemed frail, but he moved with the speed of a chipmunk. To entertain children, he was known to run around the house barking like a dog.

He died at age eighty-seven after a stroke.

Kathleen Krull: Then and Now

Then: Kathleen grew up in Missouri, the daughter of an artist's representative (her father) and a counselor (her mother). When she was twelve years old, she became a church organist. That marked the beginning of a life-long love affair with music. She also played several instruments as a child and later studied music at college.

Now: Kathleen Krull teaches at universities, but she is best known for her nonfiction for young audiences. Some of her books deal with her life-long love of music. In her own words, she is "passionate about helping to ensure that music remains important in the lives of children." In addition to her musical interests, she has written books about writers (Isaac Bashevis Singer among them), about writing itself, gardening, and even hairstyles!

Words to Know

resembled (ree SEM buhld) *v*.: Looked like

Respond

- What was the most interesting fact you learned about Singer? Why?
- In your journal explain why you would or would not like to meet Singer in person.

Activities

MAKE MEANING

Explore Your Reading

Look Back (Recall)

1. Summarize a typical day in New York for Isaac Bashevis Singer.

Think It Over (Interpret)

2. How did the tales of Edgar Allan Poe affect Isaac Bashevis Singer?
3. In what ways was Isaac Bashevis Singer's life in the United States different from his life in Poland?
4. How did Singer's childhood experiences affect his life as a writer?

Go Beyond (Apply)

5. What can we learn by reading about people whose backgrounds and experiences are different from our own?

Develop Reading and Literary Skills

Draw Conclusions About Subjects of Biographies

You got to know Isaac Bashevis Singer by reading the facts and anecdotes presented in this brief **biography.** Biography writers will often reveal the personality of their subject indirectly—through the words and actions of the subject. From this information you must **draw conclusions**—you think about what you know and decide what it means. For instance, you know that Singer was eating in a neighborhood drugstore on the day he found out about his receiving the Nobel Prize. From this fact you can draw the conclusion that he was a humble man who did not try to impress people.

Look over your KWL chart. You can use the facts in the first and third column to draw some conclusions about Singer. Drawing conclusions may help you answer some of your own questions as well as the following ones:

1. How did Singer feel about his older brother Joshua? How do you know?

2. How do you think he acted after he won the Nobel Prize? Why?
3. What kind of stories do you think Singer writes? Explain.

Ideas for Writing

Imagine that you been hired to interview and write a press release about Isaac Bashevis Singer.

Press Release Research more information about the life and work of Isaac Bashevis Singer. Use that information to write a biographical sketch that could be used as a press release about him in your school or local newspaper.

Dialogue Write the dialogue that takes place as you interview Singer to get information for his press release. What questions will you ask him? What will he say about himself?

Ideas for Projects

Montage Put together a montage, or series of images, that creates a visual biography of Singer or another writer whose work you enjoy. You can include your own artwork or images and photographs from newspapers and magazines about books and writers. Give your montage a title that describes the subject.

Feature Interview Choose someone in your school or community as the subject for an interview. Use your notes from the interview to create a brief biography for your school newspaper or yearbook.

How Am I Doing?

Spend a moment with a partner to discuss these questions:

How did the KWL chart help me organize my thinking as I read the biography?

In what other kinds of assignments might a KWL chart help? How?

Activities
PREVIEW
My Best Friend by Lessie Jones Little

What makes a "best" friend best?

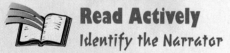

Reach Into Your Background

You may have used the term *best friend* to describe someone you know, or you may have more than one friend that is special. *Best* usually means *one* that is better than all the rest. However, when it comes to friends, you might have more than one that is especially close. Some people feel they have two or three best friends. Think about ideas and events that you connect with best friends. The following activities can help you explore your ideas:

- Pantomime (act without words) activities that friends share.
- Discuss why some activities or discussions are shared only with best friends.

Read Actively
Identify the Narrator

If you were going to write about experiences you shared with a best friend, they would represent a part of your autobiography, the story of your own life. In your autobiography, you would refer to your friend as *him* or *her.* You would use the pronouns *I* and *me* to refer to yourself as the storyteller, or **narrator.** You would share thoughts about events that only you could know.

As you read "My Best Friend," be aware that the narrator is a real person, telling a story from her own life. Keep a double-column list of details from the story. In the first column list details that only the narrator could know. In the second column list the details that the other people know.

Dressing Up, 1988 Jonathan Green, Courtesy of the artist

My Best Friend
Lessie Jones Little

Lillie Bell Draper was my best friend. We played together every chance we got. When Mama would send me to the store or to the post office, I'd go out of my way to go past Lillie's house, and I'd stand at her gate and call, "Hey *Lil*-lie!" And she'd answer, "Hey *Les*-sie!" She'd come out to the gate and we'd talk and talk until I knew I had better get going.

Lillie's married sister, Isabel, lived next door to me, and when Lillie would come in the summer to spend the day with her, I'd go over, and we'd sit on the bottom step of Isabel's front porch with our bare feet on the ground. We'd draw pictures in the dirt while we talked and rub them out with our hands. Or we'd rake the cool, damp dirt on top of our feet and pack it down tight, then slide our feet out, leaving a little cave we called a frog house. And all the time, we'd be just talking.

Sometimes we'd go walking down the railroad track. I'd take my bucket with me so I could fill it with the nuggets of coal that had fallen from passing trains, and take them home to use in the stove. Lillie would help me, but the bucket didn't always get filled because we stopped so much to talk.

We'd sit on the silky gray rails and stretch our legs out toward the weeds and tall grass and talk about things like books or boys. And we talked about music a lot. Both of us were crazy about the piano. We wished we could play like some of the people we'd seen.

We used to talk about Sunday School and heaven. They had told us in Sunday School that when we died, we would go to heaven and never, never, have to leave.

Lillie would say, "Lessie, I just can't understand 'never.'"

And I'd say, "Me neither, Lillie."

We couldn't understand "never." We could understand "a long time," or "a long, long time," or even "a long, long, long time." But *never*? Not *ever*? How could that be? We'd say, "Never, never, never, never," and keep saying it until we were almost out of breath, and then we'd laugh and say that we would never, never, understand never.

I thought everything Lillie did was pretty. The way she walked, swinging along, throwing one foot out a little more than the other, as if she were walking to a bouncy kind of music. The poems she wrote, poems about trees and other growing things, and birds. The way she sang, leaning her head back with a faraway look in her eyes, as if she were in love with the words and the music, and making the sounds come out so easily.

We built part of a city once, Lillie and I, and her sister Rosa and my sister Mabel. We built Mount Herman out of wood on a vacant lot near my backyard. The new building for Higgs School was going up then, and there were a lot of pieces of wood lying around that

Words to Know

nuggets (NUHG its) *n.*: Lumps
vacant (VAY kint) *adj.*: Empty

Daughters of the South
Jonathan Green, Courtesy of the artist

nobody wanted, blocks of wood in all kinds of shapes, squares, triangles, rectangles. We used them to build the part of Portsmouth, Virginia, that I had lived in when I was little.

Every day we worked on it. We built Glasgow Street, that long street with avenues running across it. We built stores and houses, my house on Douglas Avenue and my Aunt Ada's on Mount Vernon Avenue. And Mount Herman Baptist Church and Mount Herman School. Sometimes something would fall over, but we'd stand it up again.

At night I would think about what we were going to build the next day. I'd think about the real Mount Herman and try to remember every little thing about it. Lillie had never seen it, but once she said to me, "Lessie, when I'm in bed at night, I think about Mount Herman and almost believe I live there." One night she even dreamed about it.

When we finished, we let the city stand for a few days, then we tore it down and took the wooden blocks home for our mothers to use in our cookstoves.

Lillie and I had our lives all planned out. We were going to be schoolteachers. I was going to be just like Miss Estee Riddick, stick a pencil in my hair and walk up and down the classroom aisles calling out spelling words to my students. I would pronounce each syllable of every word just the way Miss Estee did.

But first we were going to college. We were going to Hampton Institute and be room-mates, and we would make ninety-five to a hundred in all of our subjects. We even knew what kind of clothes we would have. Lillie wanted to look girlish. She said she didn't like "grownish-looking" clothes. But I wanted to dress like the young women. I was going to have pleated skirts in all colors, and shirt-waists to match, jersey dresses with white piqué[1] collars, high-topped shoes in black and brown. For sitting around in our room, study-ing, I would have a wide-sleeved kimono like the one I had seen in the National Bellas Hess catalog, pink crepe[2] with green and white umbrellas scattered all over it.

We never did get to Hampton, but we sure had all our plans made. I was a few years older than Lillie was, but we didn't stop to worry about how we would manage to go to college at the same time. We were going to be roommates at Hampton Institute, and that was all there was to it. After all, we were best friends.

---

1. piqué (pee KAY) *adj.*: Made of cotton cloth with ridges like corduroy.
2. crepe (KRAYP) *n.*: Thin, crinkled cloth.

Respond

- Which event in the story was it easiest for you to relate to? Why?
- Sketch or jot down details about a scene that reminded you of you and your friends.

Lessie Jones Little

What could be more exciting than writing your own autobiography? For Lessie Jones Little, the answer is writing a three-generation autobiography with your moth-er, Pattie Ridley Jones, and your daughter, the award-winning writer and poet Eloise Greenfield. These women tell about their childhood memories and, at the same time, share a personal history of African American life from before the turn of the century up to the recent past.

Activities
MAKE MEANING

Explore Your Reading
Look Back (Recall)

1. Who is the narrator of this autobiographical account?

Think It Over (Interpret)

2. Why is the idea of *never* difficult for these best friends to understand?
3. What makes these two girls best friends? Which details in the story support your response?

Go Beyond (Apply)

4. Explain how the narrator's experiences compare and contrast with your definition of a best friend.

Develop Reading and Literary Skills
Understand Narrator of Autobiography

In an **autobiography,** the **narrator** tells the story of his or her own life. As you read "My Best Friend" you noted details that only the narrator could know about her own life. You also noted details that other characters might know. For example, Rosa or Mabel could have written about building a city from wood blocks in a vacant lot one summer with their sisters, but only the narrator remembers that she lay awake at night planning the next day's building.

Compare the lists you made while reading.

1. List two details you discovered in conversations between the narrator and Lillie Bell.
2. List two details that only the narrator could have known.
3. List two details that you could have learned if someone besides Lessie Jones Little had told the story.
4. Which details gave the best picture of the girls' friendship? Why?

Ideas for Writing

When you write about your friends, as Lessie Jones Little did, you reveal a lot about yourself, too.

Author Description   Write a description of Lessie Jones Little based on what you've learned in this autobiographical account. Think about what her actions and feelings, as well as what she says, reveal about her.

Friendship Memoir   A memoir is the story of one event, person, or place in someone's life story. Describe your thoughts, feelings, and reactions in a written memoir about a friend. Remember to use the pronouns *I* or *me* to refer to yourself. Include details that help readers get to know you and relate to your experience.

Ideas for Projects

Friendship Collage   Choose a passage or quotation from this autobiographical sketch and create a friendship collage to illustrate it. Use your own artwork or pictures, words, and photographs.

Comic Strip   Create a comic strip based on a humorous dialogue between two friends. For instance, Lillie and her friend have a conversation about *never*. First they say they can't understand *never;* then they say they will *never* understand *never!*

How Am I Doing?
Respond to these questions in your journal:
Which details from the autobiography do I remember best? Why?

What work that I did showed my understanding of this selection?

What Are Friends For?

Student Art **Untitled**
Walt Whitman High School
Bethesda, Maryland

In Teaching a Friend to Fly

Student Writing Georgia Gelmis
Saint Ann's Middle School
Brooklyn, New York

In teaching a friend to fly
I learned that not everyone has wings.

We stood on the air
And looked up
And looked down.
I flew beautifully,
Gracefully,
Artfully.

My friend had trouble.
"Spread yourself out," I told him.
"Your arms are your primaries and your fingers
are your secondaries.
Your thoughts are your engine,
And your laughter is your wings."

Activities PREVIEW
Zlateh the Goat   by Isaac Bashevis Singer

How do friends help you survive?

Read Actively
Identify Cause and Effect

Most circumstances in the situations you just considered occurred for a **cause**, or reason. Each circumstance or event also has an **effect**, or result. For instance, the *cause* of your helping a friend to study is that the friend is not doing well in class. The *effect* of your helping a friend to study is that your friend will probably do better.

As they do in real life, events in stories take place for a reason, or cause. Most also have an effect. Understanding the causes and effects makes the story more meaningful because you understand the relationships between events.

As you read this story, use a chart like the one shown to jot down the cause-and-effect relationships you find.

Reach Into Your Background

You've probably read stories about rescues in which one friend saves another's life. Even if you never have to do something as dramatic as that, you and your friends help one another every day. You may listen when a friend has a problem. You may offer your time or talent to help a friend. For instance, you might help a friend study a subject that he or she doesn't know as well as you do. With a partner or a small group, discover ways friends can help one another by doing one or both of the following activities:

• Share songs, movies, or books about situations in which friends help one another.
• Role-play situations in which one friend helps the other.

Cause of	Event	Effect of

Zlateh the Goat

Isaac Bashevis Singer

At Hanukkah[1] time the road from the village to the town is usually covered with snow, but this year the winter had been a mild one. Hanukkah had almost come, yet little snow had fallen. The sun shone most of the time. The peasants complained that because of the dry weather there would be a poor harvest of winter grain. New grass sprouted, and the peasants sent their cattle out to pasture.

For Reuven the furrier it was a bad year, and after long hesitation he decided to sell Zlateh the goat. She was old and gave little milk. Feivel the town butcher had offered eight gulden[2] for her. Such a sum would buy Hanukkah candles, potatoes and oil for pancakes, gifts for the children, and other holiday necessaries for the house. Reuven told his oldest boy Aaron to take the goat to town.

Aaron understood what taking the goat to Feivel meant, but had to obey his father. Leah, his mother, wiped the tears from her eyes when she heard the news. Aaron's younger sisters, Anna and Miriam, cried loudly. Aaron put on his quilted jacket and a cap with earmuffs, bound a rope around Zlateh's neck, and took along two slices of bread with cheese to eat on the road. Aaron was supposed to deliver the goat by evening, spend the night at the butcher's, and return the next day with the money.

---

1. Hanukkah (HAH noo kah) *n.*: The Jewish "Festival of Lights," usually celebrated during December.

2. gulden (GOOL din) *n.*: Units of money.

Words to Know

bound (BOWND) *v.*: Tied

Maurice Sendak, Harper & Row, Publishers, Inc.

"In a short time their path was completely covered."

While the family said goodbye to the goat, and Aaron placed the rope around her neck, Zlateh stood as patiently and good-naturedly as ever. She licked Reuven's hand. She shook her small white beard. Zlateh trusted human beings. She knew that they always fed her and never did her any harm.

When Aaron brought her out on the road to town, she seemed somewhat astonished. She'd never been led in that direction before. She looked back at him questioningly, as if to say, "Where are you taking me?" But after a while she seemed to come to the conclusion that a goat shouldn't ask questions. Still, the road was different. They passed new fields, pastures, and huts with thatched roofs. Here and there a dog barked and came running after them, but Aaron chased it away with his stick.

The sun was shining when Aaron left the village. Suddenly the weather changed. A large black cloud with a bluish center appeared in the east and spread itself rapidly over the sky. A cold wind blew in with it. The crows flew low, croaking. At first it looked as if it would rain, but instead it began to hail as in summer. It was early in the day, but it became dark as dusk. After a while the hail turned to snow.

In his twelve years Aaron had seen all kinds of weather, but he had never experienced a snow like this one. It was so dense it shut out the light of the day. In a short time their path was completely covered. The wind became as cold as ice. The road to town was narrow and winding. Aaron no longer

Words to Know

rapidly (RAHP id lee) *adv.*: Very quickly
dense (DENS) *adj.*: Very thick

knew where he was. He could not see through the snow. The cold soon penetrated his quilted jacket.

At first Zlateh didn't seem to mind the change in weather. She, too, was twelve years old and knew what winter meant. But when her legs sank deeper and deeper into the snow, she began to turn her head and look at Aaron in wonderment. Her mild eyes seemed to ask, "Why are we out in such a storm?" Aaron hoped that a peasant would come along with his cart, but no one passed by.

The snow grew thicker, falling to the ground in large, whirling flakes. Beneath it Aaron's boots touched the softness of a plowed field. He realized that he was no longer on the road. He had gone astray. He could no longer figure out which was east or west, which way was the village, the town. The wind whistled, howled, whirled the snow about in eddies.[3] It looked as if white imps were playing tag on the fields. A white dust rose above the ground. Zlateh stopped. She could walk no longer. Stubbornly she anchored her cleft hooves in the earth and bleated as if pleading to be taken home. Icicles hung from her white beard, and her horns were glazed with frost.

Aaron did not want to admit the danger, but he knew just the same that if they did not find shelter they would freeze to death. This was no ordinary storm. It was a mighty blizzard. The snow had reached his knees. His hands were numb,

and he could no longer feel his toes. He choked when he breathed. His nose felt like wood, and he rubbed it with snow. Zlateh's bleating began to sound like crying. Those humans in whom she had so much confidence had dragged her into a trap. Aaron began to pray to God for himself and for the innocent animal.

Maurice Sendak, Harper & Row, Publishers, Inc.

"For three days Aaron and Zlateh stayed in the haystack."

---

3. **eddies** (ED eez) *n.*: Little whirlwinds.

Suddenly he made out the shape of a hill. He wondered what it could be. Who had piled snow into such a huge heap? He moved toward it, dragging Zlateh after him. When he came near it, he realized that it was a large haystack which the snow had blanketed.

Aaron realized immediately that they were saved. With great effort he dug his way through the snow. He was a village boy and knew what to do. When he reached the hay, he hollowed out a nest for himself and the goat. No matter how cold it may be outside, in the hay it is always warm. And hay was food for Zlateh. The moment she smelled it she became contented and began to eat. Outside, the snow continued to fall. It quickly covered the passageway Aaron had dug. But a boy and an animal need to breathe, and there was hardly any air in their hideout. Aaron bored a kind of a window through the hay and snow and carefully kept the passage clear.

Zlateh, having eaten her fill, sat down on her hind legs and seemed to have regained her confidence in man. Aaron ate his two slices of bread and cheese, but after the difficult journey he was still hungry. He looked at Zlateh and noticed her udders were full. He lay down next to her, placing himself so that when he milked her he could squirt the milk into his mouth. It was rich and sweet. Zlateh was not accustomed to being milked that way, but she did not resist. On the contrary, she seemed eager to reward Aaron for bringing her to a shelter whose very walls, floor, and ceiling were made of food.

Through the window Aaron could catch a glimpse of the chaos outside. The wind carried before it whole drifts of snow. It was completely dark, and he did not know whether night had already come or whether it was the darkness of the storm. Thank God that in the hay it was not cold. The dried hay, grass, and field flowers exuded the warmth of the summer sun. Zlateh ate frequently; she nibbled from above, below,

from the left and right. Her body gave forth an animal warmth, and Aaron cuddled up to her. He had always loved Zlateh, but now she was like a sister. He was alone, cut off from his family, and wanted to talk. He began to talk to Zlateh. "Zlateh, what do you think about what has happened to us?" he asked.

"Maaaa," Zlateh answered.

"If we hadn't found this stack of hay, we would both be frozen stiff by now," Aaron said.

"Maaaa," was the goat's reply.

"If the snow keeps on falling like this, we may have to stay here for days," Aaron explained.

"Maaaa," Zlateh bleated.

"What does 'maaaa' mean?" Aaron asked. "You'd better speak up clearly."

"Maaa, maaa," Zlateh tried.

"Well, let it be 'maaaa' then," Aaron said patiently. "You can't speak, but I know you understand. I need you and you need me. Isn't that right?"

"Maaa."

Aaron became sleepy. He made a pillow out of some hay, leaned his head on it, and dozed off. Zlateh, too, fell asleep.

When Aaron opened his eyes, he didn't know whether it was morning or night. The snow had blocked up his window. He tried to clear it, but when he had bored enough through to the length of his arm, he still hadn't reached the outside. Luckily he had his stick with him and was able to break through to the open air. It was still dark outside. The snow continued to fall and the wind wailed, first with one voice and then with many. Sometimes it had the sound of devilish laughter. Zlateh, too, awoke, and when Aaron greeted her, she answered, "Maaa." Yes, Zlateh's language consisted of only one word, but it meant many things. Now she was saying, "We must accept

Words to Know

bored (BAWRD) *v*.: Made a hole or tunnel

exuded (eg ZOOD id) *v*.: Poured out

all that God gives us—heat, cold, hunger, satisfaction, light, and darkness."

Aaron had awakened hungry. He had eaten up his food, but Zlateh had plenty of milk.

For three days Aaron and Zlateh stayed in the haystack. Aaron had always loved Zlateh, but in these three days he loved her more and more. She fed him with her milk and helped him keep warm. She comforted him with her patience. He told her many stories, and she always cocked her ears and listened. When he patted her, she licked his hand and his face. Then she said, "Maaaa," and he knew it meant, I love you, too.

The snow fell for three days, though after the first day it was not as thick and the wind quieted down. Sometimes Aaron felt that there could never have been a summer, that the snow had always fallen, ever since he could remember. He, Aaron, never had a father or mother or sisters. He was a snow child, born of the snow, and so was Zlateh. It was so quiet in the hay that his ears rang in the stillness. Aaron and Zlateh slept all night and a good part of the day. As for Aaron's dreams, they were all about warm weather. He dreamed of green fields, trees covered with blossoms, clear brooks, and singing birds. By the third night the snow had stopped, but Aaron did not dare to find his way home in the darkness. The sky became clear and the moon

shone, casting silvery nets on the snow. Aaron dug his way out and looked at the world. It was all white, quiet, dreaming dreams of heavenly splendor. The stars were large and close. The moon swam in the sky as in a sea.

On the morning of the fourth day Aaron heard the ringing of sleigh bells. The haystack

Maurice Sendak, Harper & Row, Publishers, Inc.

"Aaron had decided in the haystack that he would never part with Zlateh."

was not far from the road. The peasant who drove the sleigh pointed out the way to him—not to the town and Feivel the butcher, but home to the village. Aaron had decided in the haystack that he would never part with Zlateh.

Aaron's family and their neighbors had searched for the boy and the goat but had found no trace of them during the storm. They feared they were lost. Aaron's mother and sisters cried for him; his father remained silent and gloomy. Suddenly one of the neighbors came running to their house with the news that Aaron and Zlateh were coming up the road.

There was great joy in the family. Aaron told them how he had found the stack of hay and how Zlateh had fed him with her milk. Aaron's sisters kissed and hugged Zlateh and gave her a special treat of chopped carrots and potato peels, which Zlateh gobbled up hungrily.

Nobody ever again thought of selling Zlateh, and now that the cold weather had finally set in, the villagers needed the services of Reuven the furrier once more. When Hanukkah came, Aaron's mother was able to fry pancakes every evening, and Zlateh got her portion, too. Even though Zlateh had her own pen, she often came to the kitchen, knocking on the door with her horns to indicate that she was ready to visit, and she was always admitted. In the evening Aaron, Miriam, and Anna played dreidel.[4] Zlateh sat near the stove watching the children and the flickering of the Hanukkah candles.

Once in a while Aaron would ask her, "Zlateh, do you remember the three days we spent together?"

And Zlateh would scratch her neck with a horn, shake her white bearded head, and come out with the single sound which expressed all her thoughts, and all her love.

----

4. **dreidel** (DRAY duhl) *n.*: A game played with a top during Hanukkah.

Respond

- What do you think was the most important thing Zlateh did for Aaron?
- Pantomime (act without words) what it would feel like to be caught in the storm that Aaron and Zlateh found themselves in.

Q: How does **Isaac Bashevis Singer** (1904–1991), the 1978 Nobel Prize–winner for literature, feel about writing for young readers?
A: He likes to write for young readers because "They love interesting stories, not commentary, guides, or footnotes. When a book is boring, they yawn openly, without any shame or fear of authority."
Q: How does Singer feel about the fact that many people read his work translated from its original Yiddish (the traditional language of European Jewish culture)?
A: He admits that reading a story translated into English is not the same as reading a story in its original Yiddish version. He once told a friend that at least forty percent of the quality of a story gets lost in the translation. Therefore, Singer advised his friend, a Yiddish writer should write a story that is one hundred and forty percent as good if it is to be translated successfully.

The Granger Collection, New York

Activities
MAKE MEANING

Explore Your Reading

Look Back (Recall)

1. Why do Aaron and Zlateh leave home together?

Think It Over (Interpret)

2. How is Zlateh able to survive the snowstorm?
3. How is Aaron able to survive the snowstorm?
4. What do you think would have been the result if either Aaron or Zlateh were alone in the snowstorm?
5. After the experience in the snowstorm, why did Aaron's family let Zlateh into the house whenever she knocked on the door?

Go Beyond (Apply)

6. What lesson does this story teach about cooperation?

Develop Reading and Literary Skills

Understand Cause and Effect in Plot

The notes you jotted down about the results of Aaron and Zlateh's helping each other show outcomes, or effects, of events in the story. For example, Reuven does not have enough money for the family to enjoy a holiday. This situation is a **cause**. The **effect**, or result, is that he decides to sell Zlateh. These two events set the **plot**, the sequence of events, in motion. The events that occur after Aaron and Zlateh leave home are a series of causes and effects that develop the plot.

1. Choose an event whose causes and effects appear on your chart. What would the story be like if this event had a different outcome?
2. Do you consider the results of what happened to Aaron and Zlateh positive or negative? Why?

Ideas for Writing

If an event in history had a result different from what really happened, peoples' lives could have been very different.

Newspaper Article Write a newspaper account for the village paper about the experiences of Aaron and Zlateh. Use bold headlines to declare what happened. Imagine that you have interviewed Aaron and his family. Include quotations from them in your article.

Altered History Story Write a story that tells the effect of changing a historical fact—for example, if the Confederate rather than the Union army won the Civil War. Develop a main character whose life is affected by this historical event.

Ideas for Projects

Comic Strip What other stories do you know about friendships? Share those you know with members of a small group. As a group, choose one of these stories to use as the subject for a comic strip. Panels should illustrate the events in their correct order. Dialogue balloons can be used in each panel to show what the characters say.

Weather Diagram In "Zlateh the Goat," weather is almost like one of the characters. Weather is the effect of certain conditions, or causes, in the atmosphere. Create a diagram that shows how a certain type of weather occurs, such as rain, snow, fog, tornadoes, hurricanes, or sunshine. Use library or other available resources to research the weather conditions you want to show on your diagram. [Science Link]

How Am I Doing?

Take a moment to answer these questions:

What have I learned about the plot of a story by noticing causes and effects?

How can I use causes and effects to help me understand what friends are for when I read other stories about friendship?

Who *really listens to you?*

Reach Into Your Background

When you have especially good news, or a problem you want to talk about, do you go to one particular person? You may feel that some people listen better than others—and you probably would go to one of them with your problem or news. The following activities can help you think about why some people are better listeners than others:

- Chart out the characteristics of a good listener.
- Describe someone who really listens to you.

Read Actively

Recognize Themes in Poems

One of the features of a good listener is that he or she pays attention and understands what you are saying. You can be a good "listener" when you read poetry. It's easy to know what the subject of the poem is, but you have to pay close attention to understand the poet's message about the topic. When you "hear" the poet's message, you are recognizing the **theme** of the poem.

As you read each poem, "listen" for the message the poet is trying to communicate. Jot down notes that give you clues to the theme.

LISTENING

Laura Paley

I talk to my dog a lot
probably because he is the only one who listens.
I tell him things my friends would laugh at:
How I hate it when mosquitoes buzz in my ear,
5   How I drink coffee to impress people even though
I hate it,
I tell him why I like chocolate with
        syrup.
He may not answer me or say anything
10 but I know he listens in his own way.
I can tell he understands.

Respond

How do you think the speaker knows her dog is listening?

Student **Laura Paley** wrote this poem for her school literary magazine when she was in middle school. She began writing poetry when she was seven years old, and still enjoys writing.

people

Charlotte Zolotow

Busy in Paradise, 1984
Derek Boshier
Texas Gallery, Houston

Some people talk and talk
and never say a thing.
Some people look at you
and birds begin to sing.

5 Some people laugh and laugh
and yet you want to cry.
Some people touch your hand
and music fills the sky.

Respond

Which kind of people do
you meet most often?

Charlotte Zolotow

(1915–   ) has known she
wanted to be a writer
since she was in fourth
grade. She has always
been interested in how
"the sounds of the words
communicate the mean-
ings of the words."

Activities

MAKE MEANING

Explore Your Reading

Think It Over (Interpret)

1. What details in "Listening" help you know that the speaker is understood when she speaks?
2. Compare and contrast the different kinds of people Charlotte Zolotow describes in "People."

Go Beyond (Apply)

3. How do these poems answer the question "What are friends for?"

Develop Reading and Literary Skills

Compare and Contrast Themes

As you jotted down notes for each poem, you were discovering the message—that is, the poem's **theme**. For example, in Laura Paley's poem, the details she used to describe her dog created an example of a caring listener. By describing a caring listener, she is saying something about listening— she was communicating a theme.

Copy the Venn diagram into your notebook. In the section marked "Listening" jot down details that you found only in that poem. In the section marked "People" jot down details that are found only in that poem. In the center section, where the circles overlap, jot down details that are common to both poems. Look over the details you jotted down. What message do they add up to?

Use the details on the Venn diagram to **compare and contrast** the themes you discover in the two poems—find the similarities and differences between them.

LISTENING   PEOPLE

Dog listens in his own way | People laugh | People can talk to you and say nothing

1. What is the theme of "Listening"? Support your answer with details from your diagram.
2. What is the theme of "People"? Explain.
3. Compare and contrast the themes of the two poems.

Ideas for Writing

Imagine that you have been given the opportunity to create the perfect listener.

Description Write a description for the perfect listener. Include the kinds of details you might see in a job ad, such as required listening background or experience and time requirements for listeners.

Listening Guide Work with a small group of classmates to write a "Guide for Good Listeners" for younger children. Show each rule with an illustration if you wish.

Ideas for Projects

Community Resource Poster Create a "Who listens to us?" poster for your classroom. Show the different resources in your school or community where students can go with a problem.

Traveler's Guide Looking right at someone is usually considered a sign that you are listening carefully. In some countries though, it would be very disrespectful to do so! Create a traveler's guidebook that gives some pointers about communication customs and manners in other cultures.
[Social Studies Link]

How Am I Doing?

In a small group, consider these questions:

What did the Venn diagram help me discover about the two poems?

How can I use a Venn diagram to help me in my other subject areas?

How does a crisis affect a friendship?

Reach Into Your Background

A crisis can bring out the best or the worst in people. It can bring out hidden strengths you never knew you had. In stories, a crisis usually brings the characters to a point when they must make an important decision or face a challenge. Look ahead at the pictures that go with the story. With a partner or small group, do one or both of the following activities to explore what the crisis might be and how it might affect the story:

- Describe each of the two main characters you see in the pictures.
- Make predictions about the crisis they will face.
- Discuss whether you think the crisis will bring out the best or the worst in them. Tell why.

Read Actively

Identify Key Events in Plot

The pictures in a story usually show the most important events. However, you will have to read the story to find out if your interpretation of the action in the pictures is correct. As you read, jot down notes about the **key events** in the **plot**, or sequence of events. Identifying the key events will help you answer the following important questions:

- Who are the main characters?
- What is the problem?
- What crisis is faced by the characters ? What events lead up to the crisis?
- How do the characters respond to the crisis?

Frosted Fire

Sheila Kelly Welch

Over and over her father had told her, "He's not the same horse. He's changed." But Sara had refused to believe him.

Now she stomped her feet hard on the gravel floor, trying to jar some feeling back into her half-frozen toes. She reached up and gently stroked the tall gray gelding's neck.

"Do you think Dad's right?" asked her younger brother Jay.

Sara shrugged, then swung into the saddle and turned Frosty toward the open space in the center of the machine shed. Riding inside in the dim, dull light of the big shed was depressing. But the fields and riding ring were snow-covered, and she had to keep working with her horse every day if she was ever going to prove that her father was wrong.

"Easy, honey," she whispered to Frosty as she rubbed beneath his dark mane. But she felt no relaxation in the horse—only collected tension in the muscles under her. Focusing her gaze on the low jump at the far end of the shed, she tried to suppress her misgivings. Carefully, lightly, she pressed her legs against Frosty's sides, urging him into a trot. He sprang forward too fast—unbalanced and unsteady.

As they cantered toward the low hurdle, it seemed to grow into a solid and forbidding wall. She'd been working with Frosty for weeks, going over all the basics, yet he didn't feel ready. A clutch of fear grasped Sara's throat, and abruptly she turned the horse to one side and pulled him to a halt.

"He won't do it, will he?" Jay asked.

Sara shook her head. "I don't know. I decided not to try it."

With Jay trailing behind, she led Frosty back to the stables. Maybe he

CLAREMONT
HORSE
SHOW

Words to Know

jar (JAR) *v.*: Jolt or shake

suppress (suh PRES) *v.*: Force back or squash down

abruptly (uh BRUPT lee) *adj.*: Suddenly; unexpectedly

wouldn't jump anymore, but at least he belonged to her now. Officially. She'd always thought of Frosty as her horse even though he'd been foaled at her uncle's horse farm. She had been the one to ride him for two unforgettable years, winning one show after another. When Uncle Matt was offered an incredibly high price for the young champion, he couldn't say no. After all, as he pointed out to Sara, that was his business.

Unfortunately for Frosty, he'd been bought by the parents of a young girl who didn't have much riding experience. When she tried her first jump, she fell off but hung on to the reins, giving Frosty's tender mouth a vicious yank. On her next ride, she fell again. Only this time she broke her arm, and the horse was blamed.

Owner after owner followed—none able to control the now-skittish horse—until finally one contacted Uncle Matt to complain. After Sara begged and pleaded, her parents offered to buy the horse at a price they could afford. Frosty had come home a few weeks before Christmas, thin and frightened, but finally hers.

Now Sara put one cold-stiffened hand into her pocket. Amid the tissues and candy wrappers, her numb fingers located a lump of sugar. When she offered it on her palm, Frosty took it with gentle lips. But when she reached to pet him, he drew back, the memory of rough handling still too strong.

Illustration by John F. Dyess

That night Sara flopped on her rumpled bed, exhausted and discouraged. She set her alarm clock so she'd get up early enough to feed Frosty before school and switched off the light.

The alarm woke her. Sara reached for it and pushed the button, but the wail went on and on.

An alarm. A smoke alarm!

Instinctively, Sara rolled out of bed and hit the floor with a dull thump. *Get out*, ordered a tiny, muffled voice inside her head. She **groped** toward the window and

Words to Know

instinctively (in STINK tiv lee) *adv*.: Naturally; without needing to think

groped (GROHPT) *v*.: Searched about blindly by feeling the way

Illustration by John F. Dyess

touched its cold, hard surface. *Open it!* Sara shook her head, trying to clear it, and fumbled with the handle. She could smell smoke—even taste it.

The window wouldn't budge, and Sara's hands were growing weaker. *It's too late*, she thought. Then, suddenly, a powerful draft of winter-cold air burst in her face. The window was open! She could hear her father's voice, strong and sure. "Sara! Come on! Climb out!"

With trembling knees, she followed him down the ladder. Outside on the snowy ground, Sara hugged Jay and her mom.

"We've got to call the fire department!" her father said, then gave a hard, wheezing cough.

> 📖 **Read Actively**
> **Predict** how the family will get help.

"Hank, no! You can't go back inside. I'll go call from the Bancrofts'." Her mother headed toward their pickup. "Oh no, the keys are in my purse. Inside!"

They all stared silently at the house. The moon was shining; there was almost no wind.

Sara thought that the scene looked like a Christmas card—one of those showing a peaceful house at midnight with a full moon and Santa's tiny reindeer arched above the rooftop. But she could hear the smoke alarm, its pulsating scream muted by walls and distance. And she could see smoke coming from their escape windows in sinister, shimmering puffs.

Words to Know

shedding (SHED ing) *v.*: Throwing off
altered (AWL terd) *v.*: Changed; became different

"I'll go," Jay said, turning to run up the long driveway.

"No!" Sara's cry stopped him. "I will. On Frosty. I can cut across the fields."

As she ran toward the barn, Jay followed. "Here, take my coat," he offered, shedding it as he caught up with her at Frosty's stall door.

"Thanks." When she led Frosty out, Jay gave her a leg up.

"Go for it," he said.

With a quick nod, Sara urged Frosty forward. Across the wide pasture they galloped, plowing through drifts that would have trapped a person on foot. Sara squinted into the darkness. Somewhere up ahead was the rail fence that separated their property from the Bancrofts'. A fence with a gate. But where was it?

Then she saw it—a black set of lines etched into the snow. A fence. A jump. She realized that Frosty saw it, too, for his stride altered just slightly. Find the gate, she told herself. That's the safe, sensible thing to do. Yes! There it was. She jumped off before Frosty had completely stopped.

Sara groped for the icy latch. There! It was undone. But when she tried to swing the gate open, it wouldn't move; one side was frozen to the ground beneath a drift. Sara yanked and shoved with all her might. A sob caught in her throat as she sagged, defeated, against the rails.

Sara thought of the fire creeping and crackling, destroying her home. She had to do something! Using the gate, she remounted and trotted Frosty away, then turned him to face the fence.

For a brief moment she sat completely still, staring. Her tears made the dark lines of the fence run and blur as if they were melting. Suddenly her fear of the jump was gone. Her fear. Frosty's fear. It was all mixed together. She understood that now.

Sara could feel Frosty gathering himself beneath her, and then he plunged into a canter. She looked beyond the fence, thought beyond it, as if she was throwing her heart across ahead of them. And then she and Frosty followed.

Read Actively

Ask yourself why Frosty is suddenly willing to jump.

It was a smooth, high jump, with no hesitation, no mistake, and with a wind of their own making in their faces. They swept across the field and up the Bancrofts' lane.

"Fire! Fire!" Sara screamed, riding right up to the porch steps. For a long, dreadful moment the house seemed empty, but then abruptly the porch light flooded on, the door swung wide, and there were the Bancrofts.

Mrs. Bancroft ran down the steps and helped Sara off her horse while her husband called the fire department.

Later, Sara was standing next to her family and the Bancrofts, who had brought her home. The firefighters were tramping about, winding up their hoses, their work finished.

"Smoke damage," Mr. Bancroft said. "Bad, but sure could've been a lot worse. We're just glad you all got out safely."

Her father nodded. "The firemen tell me that if they hadn't gotten here when they did, the whole place would've gone up in flames."

"You can thank Sara," said Mrs. Bancroft. "And her horse. Isn't that the same horse she rode in all those shows?"

Sara looked up at her father. In the pale light that was beginning to seep across the eastern sky, she saw him smile and nod. "Yes, he's the same horse."

Respond

- Which event do you find most exciting? Why?
- Make a sketch or jot down a description of the most exciting event in the story.

Here are some questions you may have about **Sheila Kelly Welch:**

Q: How does an author who writes about riding horses live?

A: She lives in the countryside, sharing her home with five horses, five dogs, and an uncountable number of cats in addition to her husband. She also has seven children and three grandchildren, all of whom sometimes visit.

Q: What else, other than spend her time with them, has she done to show her love of horses?

A: She has edited a collection of horse stories entitled *A Horse for All Seasons* and written novels for young readers.

Activities

MAKE MEANING

 ## Explore Your Reading

Look Back (Recall)

1. How did Frosty change during the story?

Think It Over (Interpret)

2. Why is Sara determined to prove that her father is wrong about Frosty?
3. How does Sara help Frosty change?

Go Beyond (Apply)

4. How does this story illustrate the importance of trust?

 ## Develop Reading and Literary Skills

Summarize Plot

Look over the notes you jotted down while you were reading the story. These main points are the building blocks you can use to **summarize** the **plot**.

Copy the plot diagram into your notebook. Fill in the information about the following plot elements:
- the **conflict** (the problem)
- the **rising action** (the events leading up to the turning point)
- the **climax** (the crisis or turning point)
- the **resolution** (how the problem is worked out)

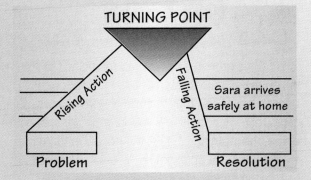

1. List three events that lead up to the turning point.
2. Summarize the story.

 ## Ideas for Writing

Imagine that you are writing a movie based on the story "Frosted Fire."

Movie Scene Write a dialogue that occurs after the fire, between Sara and her uncle. Have Sara explain what has been happening with Frosty and how things turn around. Include questions from Sara's uncle that help reveal the problem and how it is resolved.

Story Board Create a story board for the beginning of the movie to show the events in Frosty's early life that created the problem in this story. Remember to show events in the order in which they happened. Write captions that explain the action of each of the frames in your story board.

Ideas for Projects

Animal Helpers Find out how animals work in teams with humans. For example, find out about seeing-eye dogs, cow ponies, rescue dogs, and others. Create a booklet that gives a brief description of each team and a photograph or illustration. If possible, include interviews with the human members of the team.

Information Chart Contact an organization in your area that works to prevent animal abuse. Create a chart that shows its structure, activities, funding, and other information of interest.

How Am I Doing?

Answer these questions and then compare responses with a partner:

How did the plot diagram help me understand the story?

In what other subjects do I have to follow events in the correct order? Why?

The Friends of Kwan Ming   by Paul Yee
A Story of How a Wall Stands   by Simon J. Ortiz

Why do friends need one another?

Reach Into Your Background

You have probably heard the expression *for example*. Perhaps your family or teachers have asked you to "set a good example" for others. In math class, you often see completed problems that are offered as examples of how to do the work. An example is a way of *showing* rather than *telling* what is expected. The following activities can help you think about why examples are used to help us understand new ideas. Do one or both activities with a small group.

• Play an advanced game of Simon Says. Give your directions quickly and make them different from your actions. Notice how often your group does what you *do* instead of what you *say*.

• Discuss whether it is easier to be shown how something is done or be told how to do it. Use examples from your own experience.

Read Actively
Observe Characters' Behavior

You've probably discovered the benefit of having an example to follow. Writers know about this benefit, too! When they want to give you a message, they will often show you through the actions of the **characters**—that is, the people in the stories. They are an example. You can **observe**, or watch, the characters' behavior to understand what the writer is trying to communicate.

As you read the selections, jot down notes about the behavior of the characters. Ask yourself why the writer has the characters act in such a way.

THE FRIENDS OF KWAN MING

Paul Yee

When his father died, the peasant Kwan Ming was forced to sell his little plot of paddy[1] and the old family house to pay for the burial. After the funeral, Kwan Ming looked around at the banana trees surrounding his village, and saw that he had nothing left to his name—not even one chipped roof tile. He had just enough money to buy a steamship ticket to the New World, where he had heard jobs were plentiful.

"I can start a new life there," he told his mother. "I will send money home."

The voyage lasted six weeks, over rocky waves and through screaming storms. Kwan Ming huddled together with hundreds of other Chinese deep in the ship's hold.[2] There he became fast friends with Chew Lap, Tam Yim and Wong Foon—men from neighboring villages. If one friend took sick, the others fetched him food and water. If one friend had bad luck gambling, the others lent him money to recover his losses. Together

Illustration from *The Friends of Kwan Ming*

Simon Ng
Simon & Schuster

---

1. **paddy** (PAD ee) *n*.: A rice field.
2. **ship's hold:** The inside of the ship, under the decks, where cargo is usually carried.

the three men ate, told jokes, and shared their dreams for the future.

When they arrived in the New World, everyone scattered throughout the port city to search for work. Kwan Ming hurried to the warehouse district, to the train station, and to the waterfront, but doors slammed in his face because he was Chinese. So he went to every store and laundry in Chinatown, and to every farm outside town. But there was not a job to be found anywhere, for there were too many men looking for work in a country that was still too young.

Every night Kwan Ming trudged back to the inn where he was staying with his three friends. Like him, they, too, had been searching for work but had found nothing. Every night, as they ate their meager meal of rice dotted with soya sauce, the friends shared information about the places they had visited and the people they had met. And every night Kwan Ming worried more and more about his mother, and how she was faring.

"If I don't find work soon, I'm going back to China," Chew Lap declared one evening.

"What for, fool?" asked Tam Yim. "Things are worse there!"

"But at least I will be with my family!" retorted Chew Lap.

"Your family needs money for food more than they need your company," Wong Foon commented. "Don't forget that."

Then a knock was heard at the door, and the innkeeper pushed his way into the tiny attic room.

"Good news!" he cried out. "I have found a job for each of you!"

The men leapt eagerly to their feet.

"Three of the jobs are well-paying and decent," announced the innkeeper. "But the fourth job is, well . . ." He coughed sadly.

📖 **Read Actively**
Predict which of the men will get the worst job.

For the first time since they had met, the four men eyed one another warily, like four hungry cats about to pounce on a bird.

"The biggest bakery in Chinatown needs a worker," said the innkeeper. "You'll always be warm next to the oven. Who will go?"

"You go, Chew Lap," Kwan Ming said firmly. "Your parents are ill and need money for medicine."

"The finest tailor in Chinatown wants an apprentice,"[3] continued the innkeeper. "The man who takes this job will be able to throw away those thin rags you wear."

"That's for you, Tam Yim," declared Kwan Ming. "You have four little ones waiting for food in China."

"The best shoemaker in Chinatown needs an assistant," said the innkeeper. "He pays good wages. Who wants to cut leather and stitch boots?"

"You go, Wong Foon," Kwan Ming stated. "You said the roof of your house in China needs repair. Better get new tiles before the rainy season starts."

"The last job is for a houseboy." The innkeeper shook his head. "The pay is low. The boss owns the biggest mansion in town, but he is also the stingiest man around!"

Kwan Ming had no choice but to take this job, for he knew his mother would be desperate for money. So off he went.

The boss was fatter than a cast-iron stove and as cruel as a blizzard at midnight. Kwan Ming's room was next to the furnace, so black soot and coal dust covered his pillow and blankets. It was difficult to save money, and the

---

3. apprentice (uh PREN tis) *n.*: A person who agrees to work for a craftsman for a certain amount of time in exchange for instruction in the craft.

Words to Know

meager (MEE ger) *adj.*: Poor; very little
retorted (ree TAWRT id) *v.*: Replied sharply
warily (WAYR uh lee) *adv.*: Carefully and cautiously
stingiest (STIN jee est) *adj.*: The most unwilling to spend any money; miserly

servants had to fight over the left-overs for their meals.

Every day Kwan Ming swept and washed every floor in the mansion. He moved the heavy oak tables and rolled up the carpets. The house was so big, that when Kwan Ming finally finished cleaning the last room, the first one was dirty all over again.

One afternoon Kwan Ming was mopping the front porch when his boss came running out. In his hurry, he slipped and crashed down the stairs. Kwan Ming ran over to help, but the fat man turned on him.

"You turtle!" he screamed as his neck purpled and swelled. "You lazy oaf! You doorknob! You rock brain! You're fired!"

Kwan Ming stood silently for a long moment. Then he spoke. "Please, sir, give me another chance. I will work even harder if you let me stay."

The boss listened and his eyes narrowed. Then he coughed loudly. "Very well, Kwan Ming, I won't fire you," he said. "But I will have to punish you, for you have ruined this suit and

Read Actively

Visualize Kwan Ming's boss.

scuffed my boots and made me miss my dinner."

Kwan Ming nodded miserably.

"Then find me the following things in three days' time!" the boss ordered. "Bring me a fine woolen suit that will never tear. Bring me a pair of leather boots that will never wear out. And bring me forty loaves of bread that will never go stale. Otherwise you are finished here, and I will see that you never find another job!"

Kwan Ming shuddered as he ran off. The old man's demands sounded impossible. Where would he find such items?

In despair, Kwan Ming wandered through the crowded streets of Chinatown. He sat on the raised wooden sidewalk because he had nowhere else to go.

Suddenly, familiar voices surrounded him. "Kwan Ming, where have you been?"

"Kwan Ming, how is your job?"

"Kwan Ming, why do you never visit us?"

Kwan Ming looked up and saw his three friends smiling down at him. They pulled him up and pulled him off to the teahouse, where they ate and drank. When Kwan Ming told his friends about his predicament, the men clapped him on the shoulder.

"Don't worry!" exclaimed Tam Yim. "I'll make the woolen suit you need."

""I'll make the boots," added Wong Foon.

"And I'll make the bread," exclaimed Chew Lap.

Three days later, Kwan Ming's friends delivered the goods they had promised. An elegant suit of wool hung over a gleaming pair of leather boots, and forty loaves of fresh-baked bread were lined up in neat rows on the dining-room table.

Kwan Ming's boss waddled into the room and his eyes lit up. He put on the suit, and his eyebrows arched in surprise at how well it fit.

Then he sat down and tried on the boots, which slid onto his feet as if they had been buttered.

Then the boss sliced into the bread and started eating. The bread was so soft, so sweet, and so moist that he couldn't stop. Faster and faster he chewed. He ate twelve loaves, then thirteen, then twenty.

The boss's stomach swelled like a circus tent, and his feet bloated out like balloons. But the well-sewn suit and sturdy boots held him tight like a gigantic sausage. The man shouted for help. He tried to stand up, but he couldn't even get out of his chair. He kicked his feet about like a baby throwing a tantrum.

Read Actively

Connect the message of this folk tale to the messages of other folk tales you have read.

But before anyone could do a thing, there was a shattering *Bang!*

Kwan Ming stared at the chair and blinked his eyes in astonishment. For there was nothing left of his boss.

He had exploded into a million little pieces.

Respond

Are you satisfied with the way the story turned out? Why or why not?

Paul Yee (1956–) is a Canadian of Chinese descent. One of his books, the award-winning *Tales From Gold Mountain* (1990), tells many stories about Chinese immigrants who came to the New World. This collection of stories serves as a kind of archive—a public record—of the immigrant experience in North America. As a form of public record, it helps preserve the cultural heritage of people of Chinese descent. Interestingly enough, Paul Yee is a professional archivist—one who collects records—who manages archives for the province of Ontario, Canada, in the city of Toronto, Ontario.

Words to Know

bloated (BLOHT id) *v.*: Puffed and swelled

A Story of How a Wall Stands

Simon J. Ortiz

My father, who works with stone,
says, "That's just the part you see,
the stones which seem to be
just packed in on the outside,"
5   and with his hands puts the stone
   and mud
   in place. "Underneath
what looks like loose stone,
there is stone woven together."
10 He ties one hand over the other,
fitting like the bones of his hands
and fingers. "That's what is
holding it together."

"It is built that carefully,"
15 he says, "the mud mixed
to a certain texture," patiently
"with the fingers," worked
in the palm of his hand. "So that
placed between the stones, they hold
20 together for a long, long time."

He tells me those things,
the story of them worked
with his fingers, in the palm
of his hands, working the stone
25 and the mud until they become
the wall that stands a long, long time.

Respond

What person or charac-
ter does the father remind
you of? Why?

Simon J. Ortiz (1941–), an award-winning poet, has also written a documentary for television about Native Americans called *Surviving Columbus*. He is, himself, a Native American, born and raised in Acoma Pueblo, New Mexico. In 1960, he was honored at the White House for his poetry. Students in universities, including the University of New Mexico, have the opportunity to take classes in creative writing from him.

Activities

MAKE MEANING

Explore Your Reading

Look Back (Recall)

1. What problem does Kwan Ming have to solve in his job? How does he solve it?

Think It Over (Interpret)

2. Why do you think Kwan Ming allows his friends to receive jobs before him?

3. What lesson do you learn from the way Kwan Ming and his friends solve Kwan's employment problem?

4. In "A Story of How a Wall Stands," what is the father trying to teach his son?

Go Beyond (Apply)

5. What lesson about how people cooperate and depend upon one another do you learn from these selections?

Develop Reading and Literary Skills

Analyze the Meaning of Characters' Behavior

Look over your notes about the behavior of the characters. Some of them acted unselfishly; others were cruel. Still others were wise and gentle. The characters' behavior helps communicate the message that the writer wants you to discover.

1. List four examples of characters' actions that you think the writers admire.

2. How does the behavior of Kwan Ming and his friends fit the description of a wall in "A Story of How a Wall Stands"?

3. What message is communicated by the characters' actions in "The Friends of Kwan Ming"?

4. How do the father's actions in the poem "A Story of How a Wall Stands" communicate the lesson he is trying to teach his son?

5. How do these selections use examples to communicate the writers' messages?

Ideas for Writing

The poem and the story each teach a lesson about the importance of cooperation.

Persuasive Speech Write a brief speech on the importance of cooperation. Use real-life examples and details from the selections to illustrate your point.

Illustrated Folk Tale Write a folk tale to read to a small group of classmates that teaches a lesson about cooperation or depending on another person or group. Draw one or more illustrations to present with your story.

Ideas for Projects

Collage Research a culture other than your own to find out how people work together in their communities. Use that information to create a collage from pictures, photographs, words, and phrases. You might want to find out about the traditions of Eskimos, an African people, Native Americans, or people from the South Pacific. Give your collage a title that tells something of what you learned. [Social Studies Link]

Photo Essay Create a photo essay that shows how people in your community help one another. Use photos or original drawings of people working together—volunteers, fire fighters and police officers, librarians, teachers, and others who work to serve the community.

How Am I Doing?

Take a moment to respond to these questions in your journal:

What have I learned about the importance of understanding characters' behavior?

What have I written or made that I would put in my portfolio? Why?

What Are Friends For?

Think Critically About the Selections

The selections you have read in this section explore the question "What are friends for?" With a partner or small group, complete one or two of the following activities to show your understanding of the question. You can present your responses orally or in writing.

1. Many of the characters and speakers in this section discovered that they depend on their friends in many ways. Based on what you've read in these selections, what do you think friends are for? Use details from the selections to support your view. **(Draw Conclusions; Form and Support a Generalization)**

2. If you were to become friends with one of the characters in these selections, who would it be? What qualities would make this character a good friend for you? Explain why you would choose this character over another. **(Hypothesize; Make Judgments)**

3. Imagine that you were going to use literature to show what you think friends are for. Which kind of literature would you choose to write—a short story, play, poem, folk tale? Why would you choose this form to communicate your message about friends? What would you show in artwork? **(Hypothesize)**

Student Art Untitled
Walt Whitman High School
Bethesda, Maryland

you can find that show something about friendships. Attach to your collection of photos a brief essay or article that describes the images or identifies the people or objects in each picture and the reasons for the photographs you chose. Display your group's photo essay on a bulletin board covered with other items that represent something about close friendships.

Projects

Friendship Photo Essay One way to show the power of a relationship is through photography. With a group, hunt for the best photographs

Guidebook for Good Friendships Through what you've experienced in your life and what you've read in these selections, you have some knowledge about what makes a good friendship. Write a guidebook for good friendships, aimed at an audience of younger children. Arrange your ideas or hints logically. Illustrate your guidebook; then share it with children from a younger grade.

Looking at Folk

Rudolfo Anaya

What are folk tales? Folk tales are stories or legends that originate with a group of people. Folk means people, so we call the stories of a group of people "folk tales." Long ago these stories were passed down in the oral tradition which means they were told from one generation to the next by word of mouth.

When I was a child, listening to a good storyteller was entertaining and exciting. The storyteller can use his or her voice to create a mood that fits the story. The telling of folk tales was usually quite informal. We heard them sitting around the kitchen table after supper and we not only learned some of the traditions of our ancestors, we became good listeners. Today folk tales from around the world are collected and written in books.

What are folk tales about? A folk tale may be humorous, a story of adventure, or it may be a riddle. Many folk tales concern a folk hero, such as Paul Bunyan, a lumberjack whose adventures often reveal his special abilities.

The story "The Friends of Kwan Ming" also illustrates Kwan Ming's special and admirable qualities. He is not selfish. He makes sure his friends get the best jobs. They don't forget his kindness, and when Kwan Ming needs help, they return to assist him.

Folk tales almost always teach a lesson or give wise advice. The African American tale "He Lion" shows a humorous example of how foolish bragging and bullying are. By teaching he Lion a lesson, Bruh Rabbit and Bruh Bear teach everyone a lesson.

One of my favorite folk tales is the legend of the crying woman. In Spanish she is called La Lloroña, the woman who cries. As children we were told that she was searching for her lost children along the river. Hearing the story entertained us—but it also reminded us to keep away from the dangerous places along the river.

Why do we read folk tales? Reading or hearing folk tales is an excellent way to learn about different groups and cultures. They teach us how people live, and about their beliefs and traditions. Folk literature also teaches us the language, history, and environment of a people. The stories tell us what the group values. If a group admires honesty in its members, chances are there will be a folk tale about an honest man or woman.

In "The Mountain of the Men and the Mountain of the Women" we learn that in Cambodia, the groom must pay for the wedding. We learn something about the

Literary Forms
Tales

land—there are two famous mountains near Kampong Cham province, one lower than the other.

I also like the story "The Boy and His Grandfather." In this folk tale we're reminded to respect and care for the older members of our families. Even though "The Boy and His Grandfather" is set in New Mexico in the United States, many other countries have similar stories. Folk tales travel wherever people travel. As you read more and more folk tales, you will discover that many have a similar message.

We need to learn to get along with one another. Knowing the folk tales of different groups is a good way to relate to others and to discover ways we are different—but really the same.

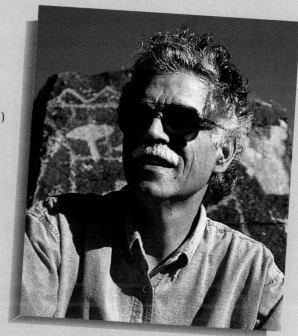

The folk tales **Rudolfo Anaya** (1937–   ) heard as a child didn't just teach him valuable lessons—they helped him become a writer. He says, "I became a writer in my childhood. That is why that time has been so important to me. The characters of my childhood, the family, friends, and neighbors, that made up my world, they and their lives fed my imagination. All cultural groups develop an oral tradition, and the tradition of the Mexican Americans is immensely rich. The stories of characters, fanciful and real, constantly filled my life. In the circle of my own community, my imagination was nourished."

Activities
PREVIEW

He Lion, Bruh Bear, and Bruh Rabbit
by Virginia Hamilton

Does being the strongest make you the best?

Reach Into Your Background

Think about characters in stories, novels, movies, or television programs who think that being the strongest gives them the right to do anything they want to do. These characters— bullies—think that because they are strong, they don't have to consider the rights or feelings of others. The following activities will help you think about what makes someone a bully:

- Chart out the characteristics of a bully.
- With a partner, dramatize a situation involving a bully in a one-minute skit.

Read Actively
Recognize Personification

The folk tale you're about to read tells about a character who behaves like a bully. This character isn't a person, however; he's an animal. Folk tales often involve animal characters who behave like people. When an animal, or even an object, behaves like a person it is called **personification**. When you read a folk tale or other piece of literature that uses personification, use your imagination to picture the animals (or objects) behaving like people. What does the behavior of the animals (or objects) suggest about the human qualities they possess?

As you read, use a chart like the one shown to jot down notes about how the animal characters remind you of real people.

Animal character	Says, does, or thinks	Human quality
he Lion	roars "Me and Myself"	conceited
Bruh Bear	talks slowly	thoughtful

HE LION, BRUH BEAR, AND BRUH RABBIT

Virginia Hamilton

Striding Grizzly, 1989
Ken Bunn
National Museum of Wildlife Art, Jackson, Wyoming

Say that he Lion would get up each and every mornin. Stretch and walk around. He'd roar, "ME AND MYSELF. ME AND MYSELF," like that. Scare all the little animals so they were afraid to come outside in the sun-shine. Afraid to go huntin or fishin or whatever the little animals wanted to do.

"What we gone do about it?" they asked one another. Squirrel leapin from branch to branch, just scared. Possum playin dead, couldn't hardly move him.

He Lion just went on, stickin out his chest and roarin, "ME AND MYSELF. ME AND MYSELF."

The little animals held a sit-down talk, and one by one and two by two and all by all, they decide to go see Bruh Bear and Bruh Rabbit. For they know that Bruh Bear been around. And Bruh Rabbit say he has, too.

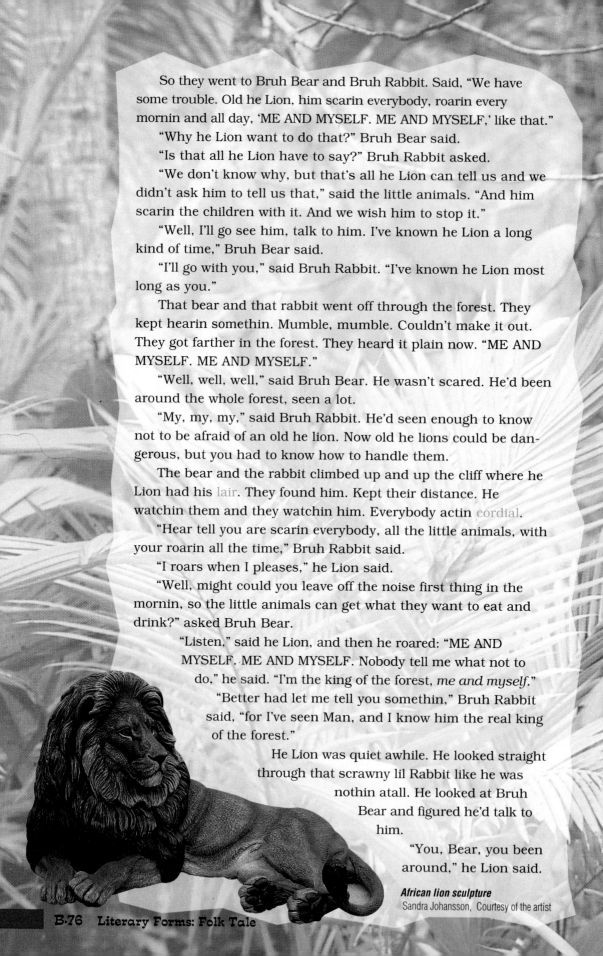

So they went to Bruh Bear and Bruh Rabbit. Said, "We have some trouble. Old he Lion, him scarin everybody, roarin every mornin and all day, 'ME AND MYSELF. ME AND MYSELF,' like that."

"Why he Lion want to do that?" Bruh Bear said.

"Is that all he Lion have to say?" Bruh Rabbit asked.

"We don't know why, but that's all he Lion can tell us and we didn't ask him to tell us that," said the little animals. "And him scarin the children with it. And we wish him to stop it."

"Well, I'll go see him, talk to him. I've known he Lion a long kind of time," Bruh Bear said.

"I'll go with you," said Bruh Rabbit. "I've known he Lion most long as you."

That bear and that rabbit went off through the forest. They kept hearin somethin. Mumble, mumble. Couldn't make it out. They got farther in the forest. They heard it plain now. "ME AND MYSELF. ME AND MYSELF."

"Well, well, well," said Bruh Bear. He wasn't scared. He'd been around the whole forest, seen a lot.

"My, my, my," said Bruh Rabbit. He'd seen enough to know not to be afraid of an old he lion. Now old he lions could be dangerous, but you had to know how to handle them.

The bear and the rabbit climbed up and up the cliff where he Lion had his lair. They found him. Kept their distance. He watchin them and they watchin him. Everybody actin cordial.

"Hear tell you are scarin everybody, all the little animals, with your roarin all the time," Bruh Rabbit said.

"I roars when I pleases," he Lion said.

"Well, might could you leave off the noise first thing in the mornin, so the little animals can get what they want to eat and drink?" asked Bruh Bear.

"Listen," said he Lion, and then he roared: "ME AND MYSELF. ME AND MYSELF. Nobody tell me what not to do," he said. "I'm the king of the forest, *me and myself.*"

"Better had let me tell you somethin," Bruh Rabbit said, "for I've seen Man, and I know him the real king of the forest."

He Lion was quiet awhile. He looked straight through that scrawny lil Rabbit like he was nothin atall. He looked at Bruh Bear and figured he'd talk to him.

"You, Bear, you been around," he Lion said.

African lion sculpture
Sandra Johansson, Courtesy of the artist

Lola Dan Ostermiller
Claggett/Rey Gallery,
Vail, Colorado

"That's true," said old Bruh Bear. "I been about everywhere. I've been around the whole forest."

"Then you must know somethin," he Lion said.

"I know lots," said Bruh Bear, slow and quiet-like.

"Tell me what you know about Man," he Lion said. "He think him the king of the forest?"

"Well, now, I'll tell you," said Bruh Bear. "I been around, but I haven't ever come across Man that I know of. Couldn't tell you nothin about him."

So he Lion had to turn back to Bruh Rabbit. He didn't want to but he had to. "So what?" he said to that lil scrawny hare.

"Well, you got to come down from there if you want to see Man," Bruh Rabbit said. "Come down from there and I'll show you him."

He Lion thought a minute, an hour, and a whole day. Then, the next day, he came on down.

He roared just once, "ME AND MYSELF. ME AND MYSELF. Now," he said, "come show me Man."

So they set out. He Lion, Bruh Bear, and Bruh Rabbit. They go along and they go along, rangin[1] the forest. Pretty soon, they come to a clearin. And playin in it is a little fellow about nine years old.

"Is that there Man?" asked he Lion.

"Why no, that one is called Will Be, but it sure is not Man," said Bruh Rabbit.

So they went along and they went along. Pretty soon, they come upon a shade tree. And sleepin under it is an old, olden fellow, about ninety years olden.

"There must lie Man," spoke he Lion. "I knew him wasn't gone be much."

"That's not Man," said Bruh Rabbit. "That fellow is Was Once. You'll know it when you see Man."

So they went on along. He Lion is gettin tired of strollin. So he roars, "ME AND MYSELF. ME AND MYSELF." Upsets Bear so that Bear doubles over and runs and climbs a tree.

"Come down from there," Bruh Rabbit tellin him. So after a while Bear comes down. He keepin his distance from he Lion, anyhow. And they set out some more. Goin along quiet and slow.

In a little while they come to a road. And coming on way

---

1. **rangin** *v.*: Wandering about; roaming.

Words to Know

lair (LAYR) *n.*: The den, or resting place, of a wild animal
cordial (KOR juhl) *adv.*: In a friendly way

down the road, Bruh Rabbit sees Man comin. Man about twenty-one years old. Big and strong, with a big gun over his shoulder.

"There!" Bruh Rabbit says. "See there, he Lion? There's Man. You better go meet him."

"I will," says he Lion. And he sticks out his chest and he roars, "ME AND MYSELF. ME AND MYSELF." All the way to Man he's roarin proud, "ME AND MYSELF, ME AND MYSELF!"

"Come on, Bruh Bear, let's go!" Bruh Rabbit says.

"What for?" Bruh Bear wants to know.

"You better come on!" And Bruh Rabbit takes ahold of Bruh Bear and half drags him to a thicket.[2] And there he makin the Bear hide with him.

For here comes Man. He sees old he Lion real good now. He drops to one knee and he takes aim with his big gun.

Old he Lion is roarin his head off: "ME AND MYSELF! ME AND MYSELF!"

The big gun goes off: PA-LOOOM!

He Lion falls back hard on his tail.

The gun goes off again. PA-LOOOM!

He Lion is flying through the air. He lands in the thicket.

"Well, did you see Man?" asked Bruh Bear.

"I seen him," said he Lion. "Man spoken to me unkind, and got a great long stick him keepin on his shoulder. Then Man taken that stick down and him speakin real mean. Thunderin at me and lightnin coming from that stick, awful bad. Made me sick. I had to turn around. And Man pointin that stick again and thunderin at me some more. So I come in here, because it seem like him throwed some stickers at me each time it thunder, too."

"So you've met Man, and you know zactly what that kind of him is," says Bruh Rabbit.

"I surely do know that," he Lion said back.

Awhile after he Lion met Man, things were some better in the forest. Bruh Bear knew what Man looked like so he could keep out of his way. That rabbit always did know to keep out of Man's way. The little animals could go out in the mornin because he Lion was more peaceable. He didn't walk around roarin at the top of his voice all the time. And when he Lion did lift that voice of his, it was like, "Me and Myself and Man. Me and Myself and Man." Like that.

Wasn't too loud atall.

---

2. thicket (THIK it) *n.*: A bunch of bushes and small trees.

Respond

- Which character in this story reminds you of someone you know or have read about? Why?
- Tell a partner what you would say to he Lion.

Virginia Hamilton (1936–   ) comes from Yellow Springs, Ohio, a town famous as a stop on the underground railroad during the Civil War. Virginia was lucky to come from a family of storytellers who passed along tales of their family experience and African American heritage. As the author herself says, "My mother was always telling things, and so was my father, telling about their history and all the things they'd done. . . . I am Black and I am comfortable writing about the people I know best. But more than anything, I write about emotions and themes which are common to all people."

Activities

MAKE MEANING

Explore Your Reading

Look Back (Recall)

1. What is the problem the animals in the forest have?

Think It Over (Interpret)

2. Why do Bruh Bear and Bruh Rabbit take he Lion to see Man?
3. What is the meaning of the character names "Will Be" and "Was Once"?
4. Is he Lion the strongest character in the story? Explain your answer with details from the story.

Go Beyond (Apply)

5. How does this folk tale help answer the question "Does being the strongest make you the best?"

Develop Reading and Literary Skills

Understand Personification in Folk Tales

He Lion is not a very nice person, is he? In fact—he's not a person at all! When an animal character talks, thinks, and acts like a person, it's easy to forget that a writer is using **personification**. Giving human qualities to something non-human is an easy and painless way for writers to point out the weaknesses and quirks of humans' behavior. In folk tales, storytellers especially like to teach lessons through the entertaining adventures of the animal characters.

Look over the chart you kept while reading. Now that you have finished reading, think about what lesson is taught through the adventures of he Lion, Bruh Bear, and Bruh Rabbit.

1. List three specific details on your chart that show animals as having human qualities.
2. Identify something that one of the characters said or did that the writer probably included to make a point.

3. What lesson does this folk tale teach while it entertains? Support your answer with at least three details from the story.

Ideas for Writing

This folk tale uses animal characters to teach a lesson about a real problem people face.

Folk Tale Write your own tale with animal characters that shows another real problem people face. For instance, you might want to create an animal character that is very shy and show how other animals help him or her overcome the problem.

Letter to the Lion As one of the small creatures in the forest, write a persuasive letter to he Lion. Give reasons why he should be more considerate of the other animals.

Ideas for Projects

Puppet Theater Get together with a group of students to make either stick, finger, or shadow puppets for the characters in this folk tale. Represent the action in the order in which the story is told.

Habitat Diorama Real lions generally are not found in a forest. Find out about the real habitat of lions. What kinds of small animals would they really share their habitat with? Create a diorama, or three-dimensional scene, that shows the features and animal populations of a lion's habitat. [Science Link]

How Am I Doing?

Discuss these questions with a partner:
Which character did I understand the best? Why?
How will drawing conclusions help me read other kinds of literature?

Activities
PREVIEW

The Mountain of the Men and the Mountain of the Women by Touch Neak and Alice Lucas

Which customs in your school or community would you like to change?

Reach Into Your Background

Most of the time, rules and routines are set in place for a specific reason. Sometimes, the reason may be safety, organization, or fairness. At other times, tradition is the reason that something is done the way it is. Folk tales often reveal the beginnings of such traditions.

The following activities will help you and your classmates think about the reasons behind some of the rules and routines in your school or community:

- Brainstorm for a list of rules, routines, and customs in your school or community.
- Act out what might happen if some of the rules or routines were eliminated.

Read Actively

Identify Key Elements in Folk Tales

There are good reasons for most of the rules and customs people follow. How would you feel, though, if there were a rule or custom, based on tradition, that seemed especially unfair to you?

Some folk tales explain how customs began. Others explain how something in nature came to be. A folk tale might tell why the squirrel is gray or how a river started flowing.

In the folk tale you are about to read, set a long, long, time ago, the young women of Cambodia decided a custom seemed unfair to them. The tale tells how they went about changing the custom. The tale also tells how something in nature came to be.

As you read, look for details that tell about customs in ancient Cambodia and features of the landscape that can still be seen today.

THE MOUNTAIN OF THE MEN AND THE MOUNTAIN OF THE WOMEN

Touch Neak and Alice Lucas

A long time ago, in Kampong Cham[1] province of Cambodia, marriage customs were quite different from the customs of the people today. In those days, it was the girl who proposed marriage to the boy. If the boy and his family decided to accept the girl's proposal, she had to pay for the wedding and buy expensive gifts to give to her future husband.

This custom went on for many years. It seemed very unfair to the young women. They were not as strong as men and could not work as hard to create the wealth necessary to find a good husband.

> **📖 Read Actively**
> Identify the problem in this folk tale.

All over the country girls talked about how to correct this unfair way of finding a marriage partner. They decided to go to the king for his advice. Now, at that time, Jayavarman[2] the First was king of Cambodia. It was this king who had united the Khmer[3] kingdoms of the south with the kingdoms of the north

---

1. **Kampong Cham** (KAHM pahng CHAHM)
2. **Jayavarman** (ji yuh VAR muhn)
3. **Khmer** (kuh MEER)

រឿង ភ្នំប្រុស ភ្នំស្រី

into the mighty Angkor[4] Empire. He had created great cities with beautiful buildings covered with stone carvings. He was a very good king and the girls trusted him to listen to their troubles and help them. But one thoughtful girl reminded the others that the king himself was a man and might not want to change a custom that profited the men of the country.

"We must think of a scheme to trick the king into making the young men propose marriage to us!" cried another girl. And so the girls made a secret plan to present to the king. The best speakers from among the young women journeyed to the city of Angkor to visit the king.

"Most high and sovereign[5] Lord," they said as they knelt before the king, "we ask you to listen to our story. We girls are such weak creatures compared to the strong young men in our country. Yet we are the ones who must propose marriage to a boy, and pay for the wedding! And we must also give fine gifts to him and his family! It is very

hard for us to do these things. Why is it that the stronger boys do not have to propose marriage to us? They are more able than we to pay for the wedding ceremony and buy beautiful gifts, do you not agree?"

King Jayavarman remained silent for a long time. He gazed down at the bowed heads and graceful arms and hands of the girls. "Perhaps you are right, beautiful daughters of the Khmer," replied the king. "But what am I to do? This is the custom of our land. How can I change the ancient way our ancestors have always prepared for marriage?"

The boldest of the girls raised her head and spoke. She pressed her hands together to show her respect. "Most Gracious and Heavenly Master, may we humbly suggest that a task be set for the men and women of the country to decide for all time who should propose marriage." The king nodded his

---

4. **Angkor** (ANG kor)
5. **sovereign** (SAHV rin) *adj.*: Supreme; ruling above all others.

Words to Know

profited (PRAHF it id) *v.*: Gave an advantage to
humbly (HUHMB lee) *adv.*: Without pride; with respect to the person of higher rank.
devised (di VĪZD) *v.*: Worked out by thinking

head. "What kind of task can be set to make such a decision?" the king asked.

"We have an idea, Great Leader of the Khmer people," said the girls. "May we tell you of a possible plan?" The king nodded.

"Call all the young unmarried men and the young unmarried women of our country together," said the leader of the girls. "Tell them you want each group to build a mountain to show their respect for you. Give them five days to complete the task. On the morning of the fifth day, tell them that all work must stop. Count the days from the time the Morning Star rises in the dark sky. That is the time before the sun shows its face, while the Night Sky Crocodile can still be seen. When the Morning Star rises on the first day, beat the royal drum to signal for work to begin. When the Morning Star rises for the fifth time, the work must stop."

📖 **Read Actively**

Predict how the plan might help the women change the marriage custom.

There were not many mountains in Kampong Cham province and the king liked the idea of having two mountains built to honor him. He thought he could stand on the top of these mountains and be closer to heaven. He could also watch for enemies from the mountain top. And being a man himself, he believed the men would win this contest and the Khmer way of proposing marriage would continue just as it had in the past.

So, the king agreed to the girls' plan. The next day, his ministers called all the young people to the king's palace. As they knelt before him, the king spoke: "The unmarried women are unhappy with our country's marriage customs. They want the men of the kingdom to propose marriage to them, and to pay for the wedding!"

The young men laughed at such a foolish idea. "Silence!" the king shouted. "Therefore, to be perfectly fair to the girls," the king continued, "I have devised a plan. Listen carefully and I will explain it to you."

As the young men and women sat in respectful silence, the king told them about the plan to build two mountains. He explained how the days would be counted by the rise of the Morning Star. "Do you agree to this plan?" he asked. Everyone bowed even lower to show their agreement.

"Then come with me and I will show you where to build." The king, followed by his ministers, who were followed by the young men, who were followed by the young women, walked along the east bank of the Mekong River[6] to the place where the mountains were to be built.

"Tomorrow, as the Morning Star rises, I will sound the royal drum. That will be the signal for work to begin here beside the river.

"You may work both day and night for the five days. But," he warned them, "you must remember: When the Morning Star rises the fifth time, you must stop work. Then you may rest until the sun shows his face. Do you understand?"

---

6. Mekong (MAY kahng) **River**: The longest river on the Indochinese peninsula.

Illustration by Holly Hannon

The young men and the young women nodded. "When the day is fully light," the king continued, "I will inspect the work myself. If the men have built the higher mountain, the women must continue to follow the marriage traditions of our ancestors. But if the women's mountain is higher, then the men must propose marriage, pay for the wedding, and bring gifts to the woman and her family."

When the king had left, the men laughed and joked about the proposal. "No woman can do such hard work," they said to themselves. "We will win with no effort at all! Let us go home to our parents and rest so we are ready to work tomorrow."

Illustration by Holly Hannon

That night, while the men were sleeping, the women met. They were afraid they might lose unless they started work right away. Quietly, they walked to the building place by the river. Carefully, they loosened the earth so that the next day they could roll big stones together to form the base of their mountain. Then they covered their work with branches of trees so no one would guess they had already started.

When the Morning Star rose the next day, the king sounded the royal drum and the work began. The men worked all day. The women worked all day, too. When evening came, the men decided to rest and drink some wine. They were sure they were ahead of the women. But the women continued to work all night. They took turns resting for only a short time.

As the Morning Star rose on the second day, the women stopped working and had a meeting. The men saw them sitting and talking. "Ha," they said, "Look at those lazy women. All they want to do is sit and gossip. Of course, we will build the higher mountain. No need to work too hard!" That night, while the men slept, the women worked on their mountain again.

On the third day, as the Morning Star rose, one group of women went to the market in the village to buy some thin, clear paper, some string, and a candle. Another group went to the forest to cut some bamboo.

"Look at that group of women over there.

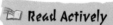 **Read Actively**
Connect the men's actions with the actions of characters in other folk tales you have read or heard.

Some are going to the village market and others are going to the woods to get out of the hot sun. They cannot stand this hard work." And so saying, the men also stopped their work to sit in the cool shade of a tree. Again on the third night, the women worked while the men slept.

On the fourth day, as the Morning Star rose, the men saw the women sitting in a close group beside their small mountain. The men could not see what they were doing. "Now just look at those foolish women! They must be chewing betel nut[7] instead of working. How do you expect to build a mountain that way?" the men laughed. They worked for a while, then sat

7. **chewing betel** (BEET uhl) **nut**: A social custom in Southeast Asian countries.

Words to Know

slender (SLEN der) *adj.*: Thin

down to rest under a tree.

Now, what do you think the women had been doing as they sat in the circle that day? They had been making their own Morning Star! They used a very sharp knife to cut the bamboo from the forest into slender pieces. They arranged the pieces in the shape of a star and tied the corners together with pieces of strong grass. Then they covered the star with the clear paper. Now the star looked like a lantern. Next, they tied a long string to their star and hid the whole thing in the grass.

That night, the women again worked on the mountain as the men slept. But in only a few hours, they took the star lantern from its hiding place in the grass and put the candle inside. An evening breeze lifted the lantern high in the sky. There it shone bright against the darkness.

At once, the women began to wail and cry. "Oh, no, what a short night this was! Now the Morning Star has risen for the fifth time and we must stop building. Oh, we have certainly lost the mountain building race to the men."

The men, hearing all this noise, woke up and looked at the sky. There, they saw the bright star shining. "Listen to those wailing women," they shouted. "Now we have clearly won the building race. When the sun rises and the king comes to inspect the two mountains, we will be the winners. Come, friends, let us sleep a little longer so we will be rested for a big celebration tomorrow."

So the men went back to sleep, and the women continued to build all the rest of the night. When the true Morning Star rose for the fifth time, they stopped and they too rested.

📖 Read Actively

Respond to the way the woman solved the problem in the story.

As the sun climbed over the edge of the earth into the eastern sky, and the land flooded with light, the king and his ministers came to inspect the mountains. The king looked to the east. There stood the women's tall mountain sloping gracefully to a slender peak.

"Very nice," said the king. "It is as lovely to look at as the beautiful daughters of the Khmer Kingdom themselves. Now let me see the work of the men."

To the west, the men's mountain stood on a broad, sturdy base. It rose sharply on all sides, but then it stopped. It was flat on top. It had no peak at all! And when the king and his ministers stood back to compare the two mountains, it was plain to see that the women had won.

Because he was an honorable man, the king kept his word. He sent a proclamation out to all the land, and this is what it said:

"From this day onward, in matters of marriage, it must be the man's responsibility to propose to the woman. He must buy fine gifts for her and for her family. And he must also pay for the wedding feast. In this way, the men of the Khmer Kingdom will show honor to the women."

If you travel up the Mekong River on Highway, past Phnom Penh[8] to the Kampong Cham, you will see two mountains, the Mountain of the Men and the Mountain of the Women. And you will see for yourself which is the higher and the more beautiful.

---

8. Phnom Penh (puh NAHM PEN)

Respond

- Do you think the outcome of the story was fair? Why or why not?
- What other folk tales does this story remind you of? Why?

Alice Lucas first traveled to Cambodia to learn more about the culture of some students in the middle school where she taught. Later, through a young Cambodian friend named Samoi, she met **Touch Neak**. Alice listened as Touch Neak told folk tales to the young Samoi. Among the folk tales she learned that day was "The Mountain of the Men and the Mountain of the Women." She wrote this English version so that her own students could enjoy this Cambodian folk tale.

Activities
MAKE MEANING

Explore Your Reading

Look Back (Recall)

1. When and where does this folk tale take place?

Think It Over (Interpret)

2. Why does the king agree to the women's plan?
3. How would you describe the men's attitude toward the women as they work on the mountain? How does it affect the outcome of the story?
4. Why do you think the women solve their problem in the way that they do?

Go Beyond (Apply)

5. How are the men and women in this story different yet the same?

Develop Reading and Literary Skills

Analyze a Folk Tale

Usually, when you read a folk tale you will find elements that you can connect with and understand easily. Explanations of animal behavior, human behavior, or things in nature like the sun, the wind, or the sky can be understood by almost everyone. However, folk tales also introduce you to unfamiliar places, people, and customs—cultures other than your own. In this folk tale, you learned about the marriage customs of ancient Cambodia and the landscape of modern Cambodia.

1. List two ideas or feelings you were able to connect with easily. Explain why.
2. List one detail that gave you a clue about the land of Cambodia.
3. List two details that revealed something about social customs in ancient Cambodia.
4. Name a place in the folk tale that you can still see in Cambodia today.

Ideas for Writing

The women in this story argue that it is unfair that they should propose marriage. What do you think about how they changed the custom?

Letter to the Editor Write a letter to the editor of the Kampong Cham province newspaper. State your opinion on the issue of the marriage custom and the contest that was held that changed the custom.

Dialogue Write a dialogue that occurs between one of the men and one of the women after the contest is over. Have one of the characters express your feelings about the custom and the contest.

Ideas for Projects

Television Traveler's Report Find out more about Cambodia, especially facts about the land, the climate, the people, and the customs. Organize and present your findings as a traveler's report that could be broadcast on television. Include visual aids such as maps, drawings, and photos or magazine pictures to accompany the report.

Dramatization With a small group create a pantomime or dance that shows the main events of this story. Be sure to highlight the problem and the events that lead to the solution.

How Am I Doing?

Discuss your answers to these questions with a partner:

What did I learn about my own opinions as I read this folk tale?

What did I do, write, or make that shows my understanding of the folk tale?

How Are We Different but Really the Same?

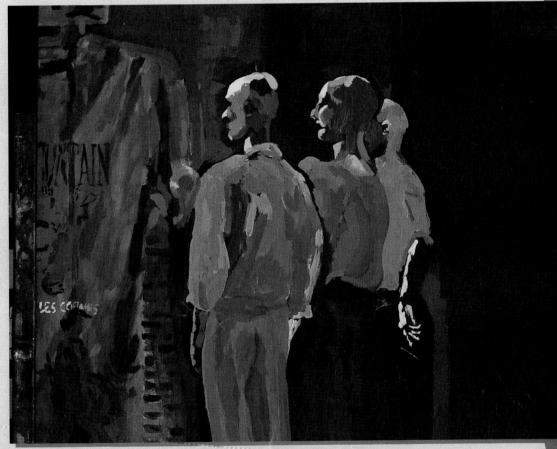

Student Art *Sale* Rob Nassau
Walt Whitman High School, Bethesda, Maryland

from *Inside Out—Upside Down*

Student Writing Karen Groene, Maggie Mudd, Susan MacDonell, and Will Oldham
Young Walden Playwrights, Louisville, Kentucky

I'm you. See us here together? There's a definite difference, there is between everyone. But I still am you. Look, I'm breathing. You, too. I've got eyes and ears. They're just different from yours. Compare us. We are different people. But we are the same.

What makes someone "different"?

Reach Into Your Background

You may look different from the student sitting next to you, but maybe you both like the same books. You and your best friend might have very different tastes in music but still share a lot of other interests. Do one or both of the following activities to explore how people can be different in some ways but the same in others:

- As a class, vote on a number of likes and dislikes, such as music, movies, books, sports, hobbies, and so on. Notice that students who vote differently in some categories vote the same in others.

- Spend a few minutes writing in your journal about how you and a friend are similar and different.

Read Actively
Listen to Rhythm and Rhyme

Like people, forms of literature can share some characteristics but be very different in other ways. For instance, many poems and songs **rhyme;** the lines finish with words that have the same end sound. However, some poems rhyme every other line, and some rhyme two lines in a row. Similarly, you can say two poems have a strong **rhythm,** or beat, but when you tap along, you find that one rhythm is very different from the other. Rhyme and rhythm contribute to the unique quality of a poem or a song.

Often it's easier to *hear* rhythm and rhyme than it is to *see* them on the page. Reading aloud will help you discover the special sounds in poetry. Take turns reading the selections aloud with a partner. As you read, tap out the rhythm of each. Listen for words that rhyme.

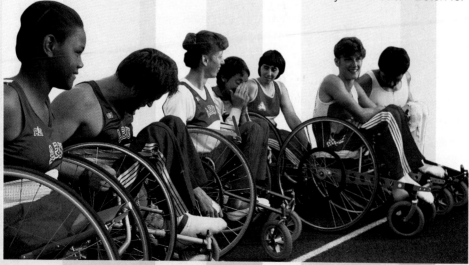

The Biggest Problem
(Is in Other People's Minds)

Words and Music by Don Haynie

My brother Bobby never listens when I talk;
Pays close attention though, and watches like a hawk.
Took some time for my hands to learn the signs,
But now the two of us, we get along just fine.

5   Bobby's biggest problem is in other people's minds;
We do things we like to do and have a great time.
Some kids stay away, but if they knew him they would find
Bobby's biggest problem really is in other people's minds.

I've known Rosa for a year or so by now;
10 We've been all around, I sometimes wonder how.
The doors and the stairs give us trouble with her chair;
It may take longer, but we go everywhere.

Rosa's biggest problem is in other people's minds;
We go where we want to go and have a great time.
15 Since this city's builders didn't think when they designed,
Rosa's biggest problem really is in other people's minds.

Angie reads to me the poetry she loves;
Hands brush the pages with the gentleness of doves.
Sings me a song from the piano clear and strong,
20 She's never seen me, yet she's known me all along.

Angie's biggest problem is in other people's minds;
We go hiking, we go swimming, in the summer sunshine.
Anyone can see I'm lucky she's a friend of mine,
And that Angie's biggest problem is in other people's minds.

25 Sometimes the biggest problem is in other people's minds;
Be exactly who you are, and you'll do just fine.
Things may look impossible, but try and you will find
That the biggest problem really is in other people's, other people's—
Someday we will change those people's minds!

 **Respond**

How does this song
affect the way you think
about what it means to be
different?

"The Biggest Problem" appeared in a special book of stories, poems, songs, and jokes
called *Free to Be . . . a Family.*
Songwriter **Don Haynie**
knows what it's like to feel different. As a child he had
polio—a serious, often deadly,
disease that destroys muscles
and makes it hard to walk or
stand like other people. However, he says he
has "a positive attitude about finding and
testing my limits."

Bein' With You This Way

W. Nikola-Lisa

Hey, everybody, are you ready?
Uh-huh!
Then snap those fingers
and tap those toes,
5 and sing along with me.

All right!
Here we go . . .

She has straight hair.
He has curly hair.
10 How perfectly
remarkably
strange,
Uh-huh!

Straight hair.
15 Curly hair.
Different—
Mm-mmm,
but the same,
Ah-ha!

20 Now isn't it beautiful,
simply unusual,
bein' with you
this way!

Say, what a big nose!
25 Hey, what a little nose!
How perfectly
remarkably
strange.
Uh-huh!

30 Big nose,
Little nose.
Straight hair,
Curly hair.
Different—
35 *Mm-mmm,*
but the same,
Ah-ha!

Now isn't it satisfying,
simply electrifying,
40 bein' with you
this way!

Now his eyes are brown.
And her eyes are blue.
How perfectly
45 remarkably
strange,
Uh-huh!

Brown eyes.
        Blue eyes.
50 Big nose.
        Little nose.
    Straight hair.
        Curly hair.
    Different—
55   *Mm-mmm,*
    but the same,
        Ah-ha!

    I said isn't it incredible,
        simply unforgettable,
60 bein' with you
        this way!

    Wow, those are thick arms!
    Hey, those are thin arms!
    How perfectly
65   remarkably
                    strange,
        Uh, huh!

    Thick arms.
        Thin arms.
70 Brown eyes.
        Blue eyes.
    Big nose.
        Little nose.
    Straight hair.
75   Curly hair.
    Different—
        Mm-mmm,
    but the same,
        Ah-ha!

80 Now isn't it fabulous,
        simply enrapturous,[1]
    bein' with you
        this way!

---

1. enrapturous (en RAP cher uhs) *adj.*: The
poet created this word from the verb *enrapture,*
which means "to fill with delight, to enchant."

    Look at those long legs!
85 Look at those short legs!
        How perfectly
                remarkably
                        strange,
        Uh-huh!

90 Long legs.
        Short legs.
    Thick arms.
        Thin arms.

***South Bronx Rebirth,* 1995** Ralph Fasanella, Courtesy of the artist

Brown eyes.
95   Blue eyes.
Big nose.
    Little nose.
Straight hair.
    Curly hair.
100 Different—
    Mm-mmm,
but the same,
    Ah-ha!

Now isn't it terrific,
105   simply exquisite,
bein' with you
    this way!

Her skin is light.
His skin is dark.
110 How perfectly
    remarkably
        strange,
    Uh-huh!

Light skin.
115   Dark skin.
Long legs.
    Short legs.
Thick arms.
    Thin arms.
120 Brown eyes.
    Blue eyes.
Big nose.
    Little nose.
Straight hair.
125   Curly hair.
Different—
    Mm-mmm,
but the same,
    Ah-ha!

130 Now isn't it delightful,
    simply out-of-sightful,
bein' with you
    this way!

I said, isn't it delightful,
135   totally insightful,
bein' with you
    this way!

©R FASA NELLA 1995

Words to Know

exquisite (eks KWIZ it) *adj.*: Very beautifully
done; of very high quality (line 105)
insightful (in SĪT fuhl) *adj.*: Having the ability
to see more than the surface; to understand the
inner meaning (line 135)

Be-bop-a-doo-bop
    Be-bop-boo
140 Be-bop-a-doo-bop
    Doo-be-dee-doo.

Oh yeah!

Be-bop-a-doo-bop
    Be-bop-boo
145 Be-bop-a-doo-bop
    Doo-be-dee-doo.

Mm-mmm!

Be-bop-a-doo-bop
    Be-bop-boo
150 Be-bop-a-doo-bop
    Doo-be-dee-doo.

That's right!

And we're gonna be like this
all the rest of our lives
155 so come and be with us
we're on our way!

HEY!

 **Respond**

What do you like or dis-
like about this poem?

According to **W. Nikola-Lisa,** the rhythm
of this poem came to him before the words! "I
started writing the book because I
got a certain beat in my head, and
then an idea. After drinking three
milkshakes and eating two pieces
of apple pie . . . I had the basic
draft . . . down."

Activities

MAKE MEANING

Explore Your Reading

Look Back (Recall)

1. List three physical characteristics referred to in each of the selections.

Think It Over (Interpret)

2. In "The Biggest Problem," what makes Bobby different from other people? How do you know?
3. In "The Biggest Problem," how is Angie similar to other people?
4. In "Bein' With You This Way," how does the speaker feel about the differences he notices in people? Explain.

Go Beyond (Apply)

5. What message do these two selections share?

Develop Reading and Literary Skills

Analyze Rhythm and Rhyme

As you read and listened to these poems, you probably enjoyed the patterns of sound you heard. These were created by the **rhythms,** or beats in each line, as well as the **rhymes,** or words that have the same or almost the same end sounds. Of course, you also thought about the meaning of the words. The combination of sound and meaning is what makes songs and poems different from other forms of literature.

Read over the poems once more. Think about what you heard when they were read aloud. If you need to, read them aloud again.

1. List three pairs of rhyming words in "The Biggest Problem."
2. In "The Biggest Problem," why do you think the songwriter has so many words rhyme with the word *minds?*
3. In "Bein' With You This Way," list four words that land on a beat when you clap out the rhythm. Why do you think those words are important?

4. In "Bein' With You This Way," list two pairs of words that rhyme. What is important about these words?

Ideas for Writing

Both of these poems have a similar message—that it isn't necessary or even desirable for everyone to be exactly the same.

Letter Write a letter to an organization that deals with a physical disability you feel you don't know much about. In your letter, request information that will help you understand the disability.

Poem Write your own poem celebrating the different characteristics and qualities of people. Use a repeated section that emphasizes the basic message of your poem.

Ideas for Projects

Greeting Card Create a greeting card that contains a poem about appreciating the differences among people. You might work with a small group of classmates to brainstorm rhyming words for the cards. Add meaning to the greeting by drawing a picture on the front of the card. [Art Link]

Choral Reading With a small group, plan and perform a choral reading of one of the selections. Divide the poem or song into sections, and assign different voices and groups of voices to the parts. If possible, make an audio recording of your performance.

How Am I Doing?

Take a moment to think about your answers to the following questions:

In which selection was it easier for me to hear the rhymes and rhythms? Why?

What did I do or make that I would want to share with someone else?

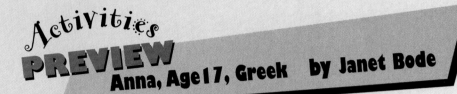

Activities
PREVIEW
Anna, Age 17, Greek   by Janet Bode

How would your life change if you moved to Greece?

Reach Into Your Background

Janet Bode interviewed many students who came to the United States from other countries to find out how their lives have changed. "Anna, Age 17, Greek" is the first-person account of one of these students as told to Janet Bode.

Imagine that you and your family are moving to Greece. You know your life will change, but you probably don't know exactly how. Do either or both of the following activities to explore ways in which your life might change:

- Make a list of facts you already know about Greece. Then make a list of questions you have. Discuss both lists with a partner.
- Find Greece on a map. Calculate how far it is from your home. Make predictions about the climate based on its location.

Read Actively

Connect With Subjects of Interviews

You may not know what it's like to move from the United States to Greece, but Anna, the subject of this interview, knows what it's like to move from Greece to the United States!

Reading an **interview** is like having a conversation. The writer reports the feelings and opinions of the subject of the interview so you can get to know the person. You can deepen your understanding of the subjects of interviews by connecting your experiences, feelings, and opinions to theirs.

As you read, use a chart like the one shown to jot down ways in which your experiences are similar to and different from Anna's.

Anna		Me
_____	family	_____
_____	friends	_____
_____	activities	_____
_____		_____
_____		_____

Anna
Age 17, Greek

Janet Bode

Greece is a rocky peninsula[1] dipping into the Mediterranean Sea surrounded by islands. The history of Europe and western civilization began with Greece, and it is the bridge between that world and Asia. It gave us a range of gifts, from democracy to the Olympics. The spring that Anna turned eleven, she and her family left their home, a placid Greek island village, population five hundred, and emigrated to the United States. Now, six years later, she is an outgoing and opinionated senior. We catch up with her after her job at the school store. Anna begins by talking about her parents.

📖 **Read Actively**

Reach into your background for what you already know about Greece.

I'm becoming an American and my parents are afraid of that. I try to reassure them. I tell them, "Look, it's me. You may not always know me, but I'm still me." When I was a little kid, I thought my parents were high and mighty,

---

1. peninsula (puh NIN suh luh) *n.*: An area of land almost entirely surrounded by water.

Words to Know

range (RANJ) *n.*: Wide assortment
placid (PLAHS id) *adj.*: Calm and peaceful
emigrated (EM i grayt id) *v.*: Left one country to settle in another

smart and strong. But now, even though I love them both, at times I see them as two children.

Take how they deal with things, how they solve their problems. Learning to be an American is very complex. And sometimes, many times, when we have a crisis, my parents don't really know how to handle it. They don't know that I am learning. The result? I often feel I'm here by myself. In the beginning, I went through a lot of things at school. The other students used to hurt me a lot. My parents didn't know how to come to me and say, "Let's talk about it. Don't worry. We understand it is hard to adjust to a new culture." They didn't know what to do, because their parents didn't have to do it for them.

Then, when I did begin to learn all these new, exciting things, I wanted to share them. I'm the youngest in my family with an older brother and sister. Neither of them went to school here; only I did.

📖 **Read Actively**

Predict how Anna's experiences will relate to your own.

Well, my brother, forget it. He only cared about himself. Like if I said something to him about earth science, because that's my favorite subject, he changed the topic and told me about his work, mechanics. He tried to compete with me to show that he knew more than I did. My sister was all involved in her work, and then her husband, so I couldn't bother her. The only people left were my parents.

Once I understood English, once I started to see a whole American world out there that I never knew existed, a world that you don't see in Greece, I felt a little distant from them. The distance grew. They would be proud of me, but they also began to feel threatened. My new knowledge had no meaning for them. This has been hard and sad for all of us.

My parents' philosophy is that, "We support you and you have to take care of us when we're old." They push me; they push my brother and sister. "You can't leave your parents out there in the world especially when we don't know English. We are your responsibility." I think that is their fear speaking and their fear that I am changing.

When we arrived in America, my brother was eighteen. At that age, he was already a man. At fifteen he had become a mechanic. There is no adolescence in Greece. You go from boy to man. It's the culture. A lot of kids don't even go to junior high school. If you're smart and you go, when you get out at fifteen or sixteen, you start work. That's when you're a man.

It's the same thing for girls. That's one place where they don't discriminate. You go from being a girl directly to the responsibilities of being a woman, and that means getting married. If you're not attractive to the opposite sex, you better become smart. Some of my best friends from my island (let's call it Thiros) are already married and one has a child. The Greek husband is supposed to be older than the wife. Women are considered ready for marriage at sixteen. The men are ready at about twenty-one, twenty-two; I guess that's because they first have to go into the army.

Of course, having a family is important, too, and sticking together in a family. Half the town where I lived are relatives, cousins, aunts, everything. My great-grandmother had around twelve children. They all got married, but at the farthest, they are only an hour away. They still come back to see her.

Up until the tourists started coming to Thiros, I think it was a pretty similar culture and life-style for centuries. Most marriages take place between people who live on the same island. You go on the outside, you have to pay for the boat and everything. It's too hard.

Words to Know

discriminate (di SKRIM i nayt) *v.*: Treat one group differently from another

It was nice to be raised there, comfortable and fun. Thiros was mountainous, except on the edges at the water. That's where most of the people lived. The best thing about the island was taking trips in the spring when all the flowers were in bloom. Horizontally east to west, it would take one hour to drive across Thiros; vertically from south to north, about four hours.

Icarus and Daedalus Ellie Tsirliagou, age 13, Greece
Courtesy of Paintbrush Diplomacy

People earn their living mostly by farming and fishing. My father used to grow things. My mother worked at home and sometimes worked with him in the small bit of land we had. My father also owned an old truck. He used it to carry supplies and farming stuff, vegetables and produce, to the market from the farms. People there aren't really competitive the way they are here in America. They don't say, "Help me take my fruit to the market, but don't help my neighbor." They realize to survive you have to do it together.

In Greece, mythology came first, before religion. When Greek Orthodox, that's a Christian religion, came in, the Greeks adapted it to fit some of the myths. And geography is mixed in with mythology, too. I love myths with all the gods and goddesses. The stories are taught in school starting in third grade. One of my favorite gods is Poseidon, the god of water and of the islands. If you live on an island that is devoted mostly to fishing, Poseidon tends to be popular. Hercules used to be my favorite story before I found out he is stupid. He's the one who is the strongest man on earth and the son of the main god, Zeus. There's Athena, the goddess of brains, although her namesakes don't always have them. And Icarus who went too close to the sun and melted the feathers off his back. One of the islands is named after him.

> 📖 **Read Actively**
> **Connect** these myths to myths you know.

Fighting with the Turks is another part of life in Greece. At some time in our history, hundreds of years ago, Turkey ruled Greece. Then in a war in the 1800s, we won our independence and regained our land. There's a whole story and we celebrate it.

Words to Know

horizontally (hahr iz AHNT uh lee) *adv.*: From one side to the other
vertically (VER·tik lee) *adv.*: From top to bottom or bottom to top

Through the Second World War, again, we were fighting with the Turkish. They have a different religion, mostly Muslim, and religion is strong. Maybe that's why Greeks and Turks don't like each other. The old people keep telling us stories about the Turks being terrible to us. We get an idea when we're children that they are evil barbarians. I don't see them that way, but that's what we are taught.

On my island they have this story about a woman whose mother was Christian and her Turkish father was Muslim. One day her father found out that she was Christian, too. She ran from him, but he caught her and cut off her head. They tell us this story, and then, we tell the next generation.

One summer my aunt, who already lived in America, came to Greece for a visit. She jokingly said, "Why don't you come live there, too." My father always looked for a better job and a better way of life. So he said to my mother, "Why not try it?" It took about two years to get all the paperwork, the visa and passports and tests before we could go. I heard my parents talking about it and I asked my mother. She said, "Yes, we're going to America." In Greece we don't have a way to "break it to the children." We just tell them. Kids don't have any choice in the matter.

Parting was hard, but I like to go on new adventures. I have a picture of me from the day we left. I had on a yellow dress and new black shoes. I was this cute, skinny little girl. We flew

to Boston and my aunt met us at the airport. At the end of a big corridor, there she was. We hadn't seen her for a long time, and at first we didn't recognize her. It was a little tense. I didn't speak any American, and my cousins who were born here didn't speak much Greek.

On the ride to my relatives' house, I thought, "Wow! This place is huge!" I couldn't believe the numbers of roads and cars and intersections and buildings. On my island the village is on a hill. They have only one main street and that is windy.

After we arrived, my parents seemed to have a plan. Because we couldn't live with my aunt forever, we found a house to rent. Living there in the beginning was kind of like camping out. We didn't have beds, so we slept on the floor. Then we got some furniture from these other Greek people who were leaving. There is a

Words to Know

corridor (KAWR i dor) *n.*: A long passageway or hallway

intersections (IN ter sek shuhnz) *n.*: Places where two or more roads cross one another

Greek community and they try to help each other. They feel for us. They remember.

The jobs were next. With the Greek connections, my father found a job washing dishes in a restaurant. My mother knew how to sew. She and my sister went to work in a factory where everybody is sitting one next to the other at sewing machines. All day long, six days a week, my father washed dishes, my mother and my sister sewed. I was told not to go outside in the yard for fear of whatever. Instead I stayed home, watching TV to learn some English.

When I finally enrolled in school, because I didn't have a report card from Thiros showing that I passed fifth grade, they put me back a year to the fourth grade. I had worked for a lot of years and I didn't think it was fair. But what could I do? I started making friends, and because they were immigrants, too, English was the language we all used. My best friend was from Cambodia. The neighbors picked on her family and called them Cambos. She never talked about how she escaped from her country, but her face had this look that said, "I've been through a terrible time."

Things are falling into place for my family, now. With my brother, I guess he felt it was time to get married. At twenty-two he went back to Thiros, met a girl, and married her. Big event, ta-dah! Before that, he'd never even dated. His social life had been to go out with the guys. His wife was sixteen when they married, and uneducated. My sister married a guy from Greece and is still a seamstress.

My father is a chef and the boss asks his advice. My mother's moved up, too. She makes

Read Actively

Compare Anna's feelings with feelings you've experienced.

beautiful wedding dresses for $5.99 an hour. My whole life plan is that I'll go to college. I will become an accountant. I

will work, save a lot of money, and then go back to school to take psychology, just to learn about it, to enjoy it. I've always been interested in why people act the way they do. I began reading about psychology, dreams, hypnosis. I'd think, why do you fall in love with a certain person and not another? Why do I like stories about vampires? Why do some people leave my island, Thiros, to come to America and others don't?

Thiros is not a place to live. It's a place to go visit, to live in your old life. Think of it as Florida! It's very peaceful, but there's not much happening. In America you have all these things. You have jobs, first of all. If you are willing to work very hard, there's always a place in the Greek community where they could make a job for you. Here, the way I see it, you have life. In Thiros, you just have a small part of it, the dream.

Respond

- What do you think was Anna's most difficult experience in moving to the United States?
- Sketch or jot down details of the image you have of Anna's village.

Janet Bode cares about kids from around the world. She has spent time as a teacher, a community organizer, and a public relations director in the United States, Germany, and Mexico. If you enjoyed reading about Anna's experiences, you can read about students who came to the United States from other countries in her book *New Kids on the Block.*

Activities

MAKE MEANING

Explore Your Reading

Look Back (Recall)

1. Describe the place where Anna and her family are from.

Think It Over (Interpret)

2. Why did Anna's family move to the United States?
3. How did Anna's relationship with her parents change after they arrived in the United States?
4. How does Anna feel about living in the United States? Explain.

Go Beyond (Apply)

5. Based on what you've read in this selection, how might your life change if you moved to Greece?

Develop Reading and Literary Skills

Analyze an Interview

Now that you've read this **interview**, Anna's story as told to Janet Bode, you probably feel you know her fairly well. Like you, she has feelings, opinions, family, and friends. She responds to events around her. By connecting your experiences with hers, you are able to analyze, or study, how Anna's experiences relate to your own.

Look over the notes you jotted on the chart as you read.

1. List three general areas that you used to compare and contrast your experiences and Anna's.
2. Identify an opinion of Anna's that you agree or disagree with.
3. List three details that reveal Anna's attitude about life. Explain how it is similar to or different from yours.
4. Briefly describe Anna's personality.

Ideas for Writing

Anna's experiences have introduced you to some new people, places, and ideas.

Character Comparison and Contrast Write an essay in which you compare and contrast Anna with other members of her family. Make comparisons based on ideas discussed in the interview, such as marriage, schooling, jobs, philosophies about family responsibilities, and so on.

Description Write a description of an imaginary place you've moved to. Include details that help readers visualize this place clearly. You might want to use comparisons to help readers understand features of this place they are unfamiliar with.

Ideas for Projects

Interview Interview a student who has recently arrived in your school. Prepare questions on topics that might vary from school to school, such as rules, sports, student interests, and other subjects.

Multimedia Presentation Prepare a multimedia presentation that would prepare a student to move to another country. Include information on customs, weather, education, and activities for young people in that country. Use pictures, videos, audio recordings, and other media to bring your country to life.

How Am I Doing?

Take a moment to answer these questions in your journal:

Which of Anna's experiences did I connect with most easily? Why?

In what other subject areas might I need to read interviews?

How does language make you part of a group?

Reach Into Your Background

When you greet the principal of your school, you probably don't use the same tone or expressions that you use when you greet your classmates. People your own age probably get a casual "Hey," while you probably say "Good morning, Mr. Jones" or "Hello, Mrs. Greene" to your principal.

With a small group, do one or both of the following activities to think about the different ways you use language:

- Brainstorm for a list of expressions you use with family and friends. Talk about how you would say the same thing to a stranger.
- Role-play conversations between different pairs of people—for instance, a conversation between a young person and his friend's father, or two teachers who know each other well. Have group members guess the kind of relationship the people have, based on the way language is used.

Read Actively

Make Inferences About Characters

Varying the kinds of language you use in situations is often the difference between choosing formal or informal language. Language can help you **make inferences**—that is, logical assumptions about the **characters** (the people in the stories). You can also make inferences based on clues in the way they act, the way they treat other characters, and the things they say.

As you read, look for clues in the way Vinny and Felita talk and act that will help you make inferences about their feelings and personalities.

A Fluent Friendship

Nicholasa Mohr

Felita! Mira, Felita, espera . . . espera un momento!"[1] I heard my name and someone calling out to me in Spanish to wait up. Turning around, I saw Vinny Davila. He was waving as he hurried over. "Hello, are you going home?" he asked me in Spanish. I nodded. "Can I walk along with you, please?"

"Sure." I shrugged. I wasn't expecting to see Vinny. It felt strange walking with Vinny because I hardly knew him or had ever really had a conversation with him. The rain had stopped and the sharp wind sent a chill right through my coat. Neither of

1. *"espera . . . espera un momento!"* (e SPE rah oon moh MEN toh): Wait . . . wait a moment.

us said anything. I kept waiting for him to say something, but he just walked silently alongside me. Finally I decided to break the ice by speaking first, in Spanish. "How do you like it in this country so far?"

"I like it." He smiled. "I'm learning and seeing new things every day." We continued to speak in Spanish.

"That's very good. Do you like school here?"

"Yes, except for my English, which is pretty lousy. I wanna work on it so that I can speak it fluently just like all the other kids."

"It must be hard to come here from another country and have to learn to speak a different language right away. You know, my grandmother lived here for something like forty years and she never learned to speak English fluently."

"Well, I sure hope I do better than your grandmother!" We both burst out laughing. "How does she manage to get along without speaking English?"

"Oh, she passed away. She's been dead for two years. She was very intelligent and could solve people's problems. My grand-mother was the most wonderful person I ever met. We spoke in Spanish all the time, just like you and me are doing right now. Abuelita[2] used to even read to me in Spanish."

"You speak Spanish very well, Felita."

"Not as well as I used to. I know I make mistakes, but I like speaking it."

"You are Puerto Rican, right?"

"Right, born here. My parents are from the Island. I guess you can tell from my accent in Spanish." My accent in Spanish was different from his. Vinny spoke slowly and pronounced his words carefully, while us Puerto Ricans speak much faster.

"I noticed that most of the kids in school are Puerto Rican too, yet many don't speak Spanish as well as you do. Did you ever live in Puerto Rico, Felita?"

"No, I've never been there. But it's funny that you asked me that because guess what? I'm going to be spending the whole summer there. It will be my first visit. I can't wait!"

"That's wonderful! I wish I could speak English the way you speak Spanish, Felita. You know I really want to learn. And, frankly, that's why I came looking for you, to see if you could help me out. Can you help me, Felita? To speak English I mean?"

"What?" I couldn't believe he was asking me to help him.

"Look," he went on, "I'll be honest with you. I've been watching you and I see the way you work. You are a good student. You're always in the library, studying. And the way you draw is terrific. Those pictures that you have on display are great. See, I've been trying to talk to somebody, like one of the other students, but I just didn't know who to ask. Then I noticed you and watched you and thought, all right, she's the one! Felita is really smart and speaks Spanish, so I can talk to her."

Vinny stopped and looked at me with a hurt expression. "Some of the other students make fun of me and call me names. I want to speak correctly. I don't want to stay speaking English the way I do now. Will you help me, Felita?"

"Me—but how?" I couldn't imagine what I could do to help.

"Teach me to speak English just like you and the other kids do."

---

2. **Abuelita** (ah bwel EET uh) *n*.: Affectionate name for grandmother.

Words to Know

fluently (FLOO int lee) *adv*.: Easily; smoothly

"You know, Vinny, they got extra classes in school where foreign people learn English. I know because some of my parents' friends from Puerto Rico went there. Let me ask for you. Maybe they might even give you special instructions because you are a kid. Tomorrow I'll ask Mr. Richards—"

"No"—he cut me off—"I'm not interested in learning any more grammar or English out of books. I can do that myself. What I need is to talk like any other kid. Not out of books, but just regular conversation. Will you help me, please?"

"I still don't know what I can do." I was getting pretty confused.

"It's very simple. We can meet after school, not each day, but perhaps two times a week. We can just talk about anything. This way I can begin to sound like everybody else."

"I really don't know about that." Vinny stopped and stood before me, his pale green eyes staring sadly at me.

"Please. Look, Felita, you say that you are going to Puerto Rico this summer. And that your Spanish isn't all that good, right? Well, what if I help you out with Spanish? Wouldn't you like to speak it better and learn to read and write it? In this way we can help each other out."

I thought about his offer and felt a rush of excitement going right through me. Imagine, out of all the kids in our school, it was going to be me teaching English to Vinny Davila, who all my girlfriends like and act silly around and drool over. The more I thought about it, the more it seemed almost too good to be true. And then I remembered my parents, especially Mami. How could I ever convince her I should have lessons with a boy? And worse yet, a stranger she'd never even met!

"Don't you think it's a good idea, Felita?"

"Sure I do. In fact I miss not being able to speak to my grandmother in Spanish, and I am going to Puerto Rico, so I would like to speak it as good as possible."

"So, do we have a deal?" I didn't know how to answer Vinny. I mean tackling Mami was a heavy order, and yet I didn't want to say no to this opportunity of having lessons with Vinny Davila.

"Let me talk to my mother and see what I can do." I could hardly believe what I'd just heard myself say.

"Wonderful! Thank you so much!" Vinny got so excited he spun around and clapped a few times.

"Hey, wait a minute, Vinny. I'm telling you right now I can't make any promises. I still have to figure out a few things and get permission."

"All right, but you will let me know soon?"

"I'll let you know when I know what's happening. We can talk in school in a free period or you can come to the library when I'm there, okay?"

"That's really great. Thank you so much." He paused and glanced at me, looking a little embarrassed. "There's just one more thing. I don't want the other kids in school to know about our lessons—at least not in the beginning. I'd like to wait until I'm speaking better in English. Can we keep this to ourselves?"

"Sure," I said. This was even better than I thought. The fact that Vinny Davila and me shared a secret made me feel special.

"I have to run or I'll be late." I turned and ran up the steps. "See you!" I called out to him in English.

"See you!" I heard his voice echoing me in English.

 Respond

- What advice would you give Vinny? Why?
- Would you like to have either of these characters as a friend? Why or why not?

Here are some questions students might have about **Nicholasa Mohr.**

Q: How does she know about a school where students speak both English and Spanish?

A: She is from a section of New York City called *El Barrio* by the Hispanic people who live there. Many students are bilingual— that is, they speak Spanish and English.

Q: Has she written other stories about either the character Felita or Vinny Davila?

A: In fact, Felita is the main character of a popular book by Nicholasa Mohr entitled *Felita.* In a later book, *Going Home,* from which "A Fluent Friendship" is taken, the author continues the story of Felita's experiences.

Q: Why does Nicholasa Mohr write about life in New York City?

A: Not only was she born and raised in *El Barrio,* she still lives in Brooklyn, New York, which is a borough of New York City. Before she wrote books full time, she worked as a graphic artist in New York.

Explore Your Reading

Look Back (Recall)

1. Where did Felita learn to speak Spanish?

Think It Over (Interpret)

2. Do you think it was difficult for Vinny to ask for help? Why?

3. Why is Felita happy that Vinny asked her for help?

4. What do Felita and Vinny have in common? In what ways are they different?

Go Beyond (Apply)

5. Why do you think people make fun of Vinny's accent? What would you tell those people if you could talk to them?

Develop Reading and Literary Skills

Understand Indirect Characterization

You probably learned a lot about the characters of Vinny and Felita as you read this selection—but little of it was stated directly by the writer. For instance, Mohr doesn't write "Vinny is handsome and popular with the girls." Instead, she gives you the information to make that inference, or logical assumption; she has Felita tell us that all her girlfriends like and act silly around him. This is an example of **indirect characterization**—the development of a character is revealed through his or her own words, thoughts, and actions, as well as how the other characters act around and talk about the character. Since this story is told by one of the characters, almost everything you know about Vinny and Felita is through indirect characterization.

1. Identify two things you learned about each character from his or her own words, thoughts, and actions.

2. Identify two things you learned about each character from the way the other character talked or acted.

3. Give a brief description of one of the characters.

Ideas for Writing

Once Vinny learns to use informal language, he will need to be careful to use it in the right situations.

Writing Models Imagine that as a friend you are going to help Vinny. Write him two model notes, each telling him about a new movie you want him to go see with you. Write one in formal English and the other in informal English.

Radio Script Write a brief radio script about a new student coming to school. Choose characters that will call for the use of both formal and informal English. Since your audience cannot see the characters, use details in the dialogue to make each character come to life. You may also want to include sound effects.

Ideas for Projects

Study Buddies Create a study buddy chart for your classroom. Survey your classmates to find out who would be willing to help other students in the various subject areas. Then post your chart so that students who are looking for a little help can locate a buddy easily.

Team-of-the-Week Display Find out about ways in which people are working together in your school. Create a Team-of-the-Week bulletin board to honor these cooperative efforts. Ask other classes to help make your class aware of situations in which cooperative efforts are taking place. Also, find ways in which your class can introduce cooperative efforts.

How Am I Doing?

Discuss these questions with a partner:

Which clues made it easiest to make inferences? Why?

What has the experience between Vinny and Felita taught me about how people can be different but the same?

What is the key to a good friendship?

Although different people have different friends, most good friends share the same characteristics. Think about good friendships you have. What makes them work?

To help you explore this idea, do one or both of the following activities:

- On your own, brainstorm for a list of keys to good friendships.
- With your classmates, develop a class cluster of ideas about good friendships.

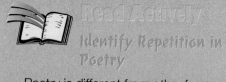

Poetry is different from other forms of literature. In poetry, the patterns of words creates a musical quality. Often poets use **repetition**— the repeated use of words, lines, or sounds— to create this musical quality. Being aware of the repetition in poetry helps you gain a greater appreciation of its special musical quality.

Read these poems aloud with a partner. As you read, take note of sounds, words, and phrases that are repeated.

Door Number Four

Charlotte Pomerantz

Above my uncle's grocery store
is a pintu,
is a door.
On the pintu
5   is a number,
nomer empat,
number four.
In the door
there is a key.
10   Turn it,
enter quietly.
Hush hush, diam-diam,
quietly.
There, in lamplight,
15   you will see
a friend,
teman,
a friend
who's me.

One Child Between Doors (Seorang Anak di Antara Pintu Ruang) 1984
Dede Eri Supria, Courtesy of Joseph Fischer

FRIENDSHIP
Walter Dean Myers

There is a secret thread that makes us friends
   Turn away from hard and breakful eyes
   Turn away from cold and painful lies
That speaks of other, more important ends
5 There are two hard yet tender hearts that beat
   Take always my hand at special times
   Take always my dark and precious rhymes
That sing so brightly when our glad souls meet

The Marble Players Stephen Scott Young
John H. Surovek Gallery, Palm Beach, Florida

 **Respond**

- Which sounds or patterns of sound do you like best in these poems?
- Draw a sketch that shows something about friendship from one of these two poems.

Words to Know

ends (ENDZ) *n.:* Purposes or goals (line 4)
precious (PRESH uhs) *adj.:* Beloved (line 7)

Walter Dean Myers (1937–):

  Q: Who are the people he describes in his poem "Friendship"?

  A: Although it isn't stated in the poem, the poet collects historical photographs of African American children. These photos are the inspiration for this poem and others he has written.

  Q: Why does this poet write mainly for young readers?

  A: In the poet's own words, "Children are the most important people we have in this country."

Charlotte Pomerantz (1930–)

  As you can tell from her use of Indonesian words in this poem, Charlotte Pomerantz's fascination with words extends beyond the English language. If you enjoyed this poem you can find more like it in *The Tamarindo Puppy* and *If I Had a Paka,* collections of poetry that combine English with other languages.

Activities

MAKE MEANING

Explore Your Reading

Look Back (Recall)

1. What is the subject of both of these poems?

Think It Over (Interpret)

2. Why do you think Pomerantz titled her poem "Door Number Four"?

3. In "Friendship," what is the secret thread that ties the speaker to his friend?

Go Beyond (Apply)

4. Based on your reading of these two poems, what do you think the poets would look for in a friend?

Develop Reading and Literary Skills

Analyze Repetition in Poetry

As you read each poem aloud, you listened for repeated words and sounds. In addition to adding to the musical quality of poetry, **repetition,** using words or sounds more than once, can add emphasis to certain ideas. For instance, in "Friendship" the words *Turn away* are repeated in two lines. This adds weight to the speaker's naming some things from which he would like to protect his friend.

1. In "Friendship," contrast the pair of lines that begins with *Turn away* with the pair of lines that begins with *Take always.* Why do you think the poet chose to begin these pairs of lines with repeated words?

2. What sounds do you hear repeated in "Friendship"? Why do you think the poet chose to repeat those sounds?

3. In "Door Number Four," how does the poet use repetition to reveal the meaning of the Indonesian words?

4. In "Door Number Four," why do you think the poet chose the words she did to write in both languages?

5. In "Door Number Four," why do you think the poet twice repeats the line "a friend" near the end of the poem?

Ideas for Writing

Both of these poems express an idea about friendship.

Help Wanted Ad What do you think makes a good friend? Write a definition of a friend in the form of a help wanted ad. Include your requirements for the job. For instance, you might include "must have a good sense of humor."

Friendship Poem Write a poem about a friend you have, or the kind of friend you would like to have. Use repeated words and phrases to stress the important points in your poem.

Ideas for Projects

Pen-Pal Letters Research a country that interests you and write a pen-pal letter to a student from that place. Ask questions about everyday life in that country, share information about your school, interests, family, and friendships.

Friendship Survey Take a survey of your classmates to find out what they think are the most important qualities in a friend. Select four or five main categories. Then have the class vote on which they think is the most important quality. Create a pie chart that shows the results of the vote in terms of percentages. [Math Link]

How Am I Doing?

Take a minute to discuss these questions with a partner:

Which poem would I choose to read aloud for another class? Why?

Which project or writing assignment will I choose to put in my portfolio? Why?

How do people without sight "see"?

Reach Into Your Background

One of the characters in this teleplay (a drama, or play, written for television) is blind. She uses her other senses to help her "see." What knowledge do you have—from real-life experience or books, movies, or television programs—of people who are blind?

With a partner do one or both of the following activities to increase your awareness of the challenges faced by people who are blind:

- Take turns challenging each other to guess what object has been placed in a closed box. You may reach into the box to feel the object, you may shake the box, but you may not look inside.
- Take turns describing objects to each other and trying to guess what is being described.

Read Actively

Visualize Events in Drama

You've discovered that it's possible to **visualize**—that is, form a mental picture of—an object without actually seeing it. You can also visualize people, places, and events. In literature, writers provide descriptions that help you form these mental pictures. In a drama, you will usually find these descriptions in the stage directions. The stage directions are almost always enclosed in parentheses or brackets and are written in italics.

Dramas are written to be *acted.* Much of their meaning and enjoyment is to be found in the *action.* For this reason it's especially important to be able to visualize the action in a drama.

As you read this teleplay, use stage directions to help you visualize the characters and actions in the play. Jot down notes on what you could and could not visualize clearly.

Blind Sunday

Arthur Barron

[*Fade in on a swimming pool.* EILEEN *is swimming smoothly.* MRS. HAYS *is sitting nearby, reading a book.* JEFF *dives into the pool. He comes up for air near* EILEEN.]

EILEEN. Neat dive.

JEFF. Thanks.

EILEEN. What do you call that one?

JEFF. A jackknife.

EILEEN. Can you do a half gainer?

JEFF. No. [*Shyly, he climbs out of the pool.* EILEEN, *feeling in front of her, pulls herself out, too.*]

EILEEN. I'm Eileen. Lee's my nickname.

JEFF. Uh, I'm Jeff.

EILEEN. Where do you go to school?

JEFF. Western.

EILEEN. I go to Eastern.

[JEFF *doesn't know what to say next.*]

You're the strong, silent type, huh?

JEFF. I guess so. [*Pause*] Uh, want a donut?

EILEEN. Sure.

JEFF. [*Reaching for a bag on a bench*] I got two here. [*He unwraps two donuts.*] Take your pick. [EILEEN *is blind, and must feel her way. Shocked,* JEFF *moves the donuts under her hand.*] Here.

EILEEN. [*Touching one*] Jelly, right?

JEFF. Yeah.

EILEEN. [*Touching the other*] Chocolate. [*She takes it and bites.*] Um, good.

[JEFF *is silent.*]

What's the matter? [*Silence*] Didn't you ever eat donuts with a blind girl before? [*Silence*] Hey, are you okay?

JEFF. Uh, yeah.

EILEEN. So relax. [*She reaches out, takes the jelly donut, and puts it to his mouth.*] Here.

[JEFF *takes a bite.*]

Now, wipe that sugar mustache off your lip.

JEFF. [*Wiping off the sugar and laughing*] Okay.

EILEEN. [*Giving him her half donut*] Will you hold this? I'll show you a half gainer. [*She walks to the diving board, climbs the ladder, and walks to the end of the board.*]

MRS. HAYS. [*Watching*] Okay, Lee. It's clear.

[EILEEN *jumps upward, flips over backward, and enters the water headfirst. She comes up for air, smiling.*]

EILEEN. Like it?

JEFF. That was great!

[*Cut to* JEFF *eating breakfast. His father enters the kitchen.* JEFF *looks unhappy.*]

DAD. Where's the funeral?

JEFF. [*After a pause*] Dad, how do you talk to someone? You know, when you want to be friendly.

DAD. You mean small talk?

JEFF. Yeah. I'm lousy at that stuff.

DAD. Maybe you try too hard.

JEFF. I get nervous, and nothing comes out.

DAD. Well, try to relax.

JEFF. There's a school dance coming up. I'd kind of like to go. But if I did, what would I say all night? [*Suddenly*] Did you ever know a blind person?

DAD. Is that your idea of small talk?

JEFF. No, I'm serious.

DAD. Yeah, in the war. A buddy of mine was wounded in both eyes.

JEFF. What did he do after that?

DAD. I don't know. He was sent home. We lost touch.

[*Cut to* EILEEN *and* MRS. HAYS *working in the school library.* EILEEN *is writing in braille.*[1] *She uses a special tool that punches dots into paper tape.*]

EILEEN. How do you spell "correspondence"?

MRS. HAYS. It ends with E-N-C-E.

---

1. braille (BRAYL) *n.:* A system of reading and writing in which letters and numbers are shown by patterns of raised dots that can be felt.

Illustration by Jordi Torres

EILEEN. Thanks. [*She finishes and hands the tape to* MRS. HAYS.] Here.

MRS. HAYS. [*Running her fingers over the tape*] Not bad.

EILEEN. Can you type it today? It's due tomorrow.

MRS. HAYS. Sure. [*Pause*] Wait.

EILEEN. What's wrong?

MRS. HAYS. The word "correspondence." You used the long form—all 14 letters. You should have used the braille contraction for E-N-C-E. It saves time.

EILEEN. I like to spell it the long way. That's the way it's *really* spelled.

MRS. HAYS. Not in braille.

EILEEN. Braille is for blind people!

MRS. HAYS. Look, I know you want to be just like everybody else, Lee. But you're not.

[EILEEN *pretends to search for something.*]

What are you looking for?

EILEEN. My tin cup and pencils.

MRS. HAYS. Come on. You know what I mean.

EILEEN. [*Pretending to be a blind beggar*] Won't you help a poor blind girl?

MRS. HAYS. Eileen, be serious. Sometimes you go too far trying to be independent.

[*A bell rings.*]

EILEEN. I've got to go. Between classes is the best time for begging.

MRS. HAYS. [*Laughing*] You're a nut. You know that?

EILEEN. [*Smiling*] Yeah.

[*Cut to* EILEEN, PAM, *and* MARGE *in a classroom. The school day is over, and the other students are leaving.*]

PAM. I think it's stupid spending all that money for decorations.

MARGE. I don't. How often do we have a dance with Western? Once a year! And it should look nice.

PAM. But we could get a better band for that money. Music is more important than crepe paper and stuff.

EILEEN. I agree. But then I'm not one to judge decorations.

PAM. When I go to a dance, I like to *dance*— not look at decorations. So does Mark.

MARGE. You got a date with him?

PAM. [*Happy*] Yeah. He asked me last night.

MARGE. I'm going with Erik. Why don't we double?

EILEEN. Why don't we triple? I'm going with Robert Redford.

[MARGE *and* PAM *suddenly feel guilty for talking about having dates in front of* EILEEN.]

Why the sudden silence? Don't you believe me?

PAM. Come on, Eileen. Don't joke.

EILEEN. Don't worry. I didn't want a date anyway.

[*Cut to* EILEEN *walking home, using her cane. At a corner, she waits for the traffic light to change.* JEFF *sees her and hurries up to her.*]

JEFF. Hi.

EILEEN. Oh, hi.

JEFF. Remember me?

EILEEN. I think so. Say some more.

JEFF. Uh, the light just changed. Can I help you across the street?

EILEEN. [*Nicely*] No, thanks. I can manage. [*She crosses, and* JEFF *follows. She comes to the opposite curb.*]

JEFF. You're at the curb.

EILEEN. Now I know who you are—Fido, the guide dog.

JEFF. [*Hurt*] I was just trying to help.

EILEEN. I'm sorry. It's just that I like to manage by myself. You're the boy I met at the pool, right?

JEFF. Yeah.

EILEEN. You said you go to Western. What are you doing over here?

JEFF. Uh, I had an errand to do.

EILEEN. Well, nice seeing you. [*She starts to walk on.*]

JEFF. My errand is done. Um, could I buy you a hamburger or something?

EILEEN. [*Smiling*] Sure. That would be nice.

[*Cut to a hamburger place.* JEFF *and* EILEEN *sit in a booth.*]

JEFF. [*Trying to make conversation*] Well, here we are.

EILEEN. Yeah.

JEFF. Nice place.

EILEEN. Yeah.

[*A* WAITER *comes to take their order. He sees* EILEEN'S *cane and realizes she's blind.*]

WAITER. [*To* JEFF] What will you have?

JEFF. A burger and a chocolate malt.

WAITER. And what will she have?

EILEEN. [*Angry*] She will have a cheeseburger, a vanilla shake, and french fries.

WAITER. [*Shrugging*] Okay, okay. [*He leaves.*]

EILEEN. That makes me mad! Blind people aren't supposed to know what they want. Sometimes people ask me the dumbest things.

JEFF. Like what?

EILEEN. Like, how do you find your mouth with your fork? Or, do you sleep with your eyes open or closed?

JEFF. No.

EILEEN. Yeah. [*Pause*] I was born blind, in case you're wondering.

[*The* WAITER *brings their food, then leaves.* JEFF *watches* EILEEN *feel, then arrange her dishes.*]

JEFF. Can I help?

EILEEN. No, thanks. Here's how I manage my dishes. This table is a clock.

JEFF. Huh?

EILEEN. My cheeseburger is here at 12:00. My vanilla shake is at 2:00. And my fries are at 9:00.

JEFF. That's neat.

EILEEN. Where's the salt?

JEFF. [*After a pause*] At 11:00.

EILEEN. [*Finding it*] Thanks.

[*Cut to* EILEEN *and* JEFF *walking along the street.*]

EILEEN. What color are your eyes?

JEFF. Blue.

EILEEN. Color is the hardest thing.

JEFF. What do you mean?

_____
2. sonar: Stands for **so**und **n**avigation **a**nd **r**anging; objects are located by sending out high frequency sound waves and measuring the vibrations that are bounced back.

EILEEN. It's the hardest thing to imagine. [*Her cane begins to beep as they come near a parked bicycle.*]

JEFF. How come your cane is beeping?

EILEEN. It warns me when there's something in front of me. It's a sonar[2] cane. I hate it.

JEFF. Why?

EILEEN. When people see it, they know right away I'm blind. It's so *obvious*.

JEFF. Oh.

EILEEN. Another thing I hate is when people talk extra loud to me, like you do.

JEFF. I do?

EILEEN. I'm afraid so. People tend to do that. I may be blind, but I can hear okay.

JEFF. [*Speaking softer*] I'm sorry.

EILEEN. That's okay. I guess I take getting used to. [*She stops.*] This is where I live. Want to come in?

JEFF. Uh, no, thanks. I guess I better get home.

EILEEN. I had fun.

JEFF. Me, too.

[*Cut to* JEFF *and* EILEEN *walking through a park the next Saturday. Then we see them feeding some animals in the park zoo, and we see them riding a two-seater bicycle, which they've rented. Next we see them talking quietly.*]

EILEEN. Hey, do me a favor?

JEFF. Sure.

EILEEN. Is it okay if I feel what your face looks like?

JEFF. Okay.

[*She runs her hand over his face. He tries to be casual.*]

Well?

EILEEN. Your nose is kind of big.

Illustration by Jordi Torres

JEFF. Thanks a lot.

EILEEN. And your ears stick out.

JEFF. No, they don't.

EILEEN. [*Smiling*] A little.

JEFF. Well, not so you'd notice. [*He smiles.*]

EILEEN. [*Touching his mouth*] That's a nice smile.

JEFF. Glad you like *something.*

EILEEN. All in all, it's a nice face.

JEFF. Thanks. You had me worried there for a while.

[*Cut to* JEFF *and his father having breakfast.*]

JEFF. You know that dance I was telling you about?

DAD. Yeah.

JEFF. Well, it's a pretty important dance. I've been thinking of taking someone.

DAD. Who? That girl you've been seeing?

JEFF. Yeah, Eileen. But, as I told you, she's blind.

DAD. So?

JEFF. I feel funny about asking a blind girl to a dance.

DAD. Why?

JEFF. For one thing, I'm a terrible dancer. I'd

probably trample her to death.

DAD. That would be a problem with any girl you took, wouldn't it?

JEFF. Yeah, but it would be worse for her. She couldn't defend herself as well.

DAD. [*Smiling slightly*] I'm not so sure about that. What else?

JEFF. Suppose I had to leave her—to go to the john? Suppose someone didn't know she was blind and wanted to cut in on me. Suppose she wanted to go to the john. Who would take her? There would be *millions* of problems!

DAD. Well, I expect each could be handled.

JEFF. You don't understand!

DAD. You make her sound completely helpless. Is she really like that?

JEFF. No.

DAD. What's *really* bothering you?

JEFF. [*After a pause*] Everyone would stare at us. They'd think I was desperate for a date. They'd think only a blind girl would go out with me.

DAD. [*Quietly*] You're ashamed to be seen with her.

[JEFF *nods "yes."*]

Yet you enjoy her company. You have fun together.

JEFF. Yes.

DAD. [*After a pause*] I guess you don't have a very good opinion of yourself.

JEFF. Huh?

DAD. What other people might think of you seems more important than what you think. Right?

JEFF. I don't know.

DAD. Think about it.

JEFF. Okay.

[*Cut to* EILEEN *and* MRS. HAYS *working at a training center for blind people.* EILEEN *looks up from her braille.*]

EILEEN. If I could see just one thing, do you know what it would be?

MRS. HAYS. What?

EILEEN. My face.

MRS. HAYS. You have a nice face.

EILEEN. Then why don't I have dates? I have friends, but boys don't ask me out.

MRS. HAYS. What about Jeff?

EILEEN. He's—well, more like a friend. [*Pause*] I used to think boys didn't ask me out because I'm blind. I thought that sort of turned boys off.

MRS. HAYS. That should be less of a problem as you get older. The boys you meet later will be more mature.

EILEEN. Suppose it isn't that. Suppose I'm ugly.

MRS. HAYS. You're not. You're very attractive.

EILEEN. But how do I *know*? Look, I'm just trying to face the truth. Isn't that what you keep telling me to do?

MRS. HAYS. Yes, and I'm telling you the truth.

[*Cut to the swimming pool.* EILEEN, MARGE, *and* PAM *are in bathing suits beside the pool.* MRS. HAYS *is nearby.*]

EILEEN. [*To* MARGE *and* PAM] You know that boy I've been seeing?

MARGE. Yeah, Jeff.

EILEEN. Yeah. He says he likes dancing.

MARGE. Yeah? He looks kind of clumsy to me.

EILEEN. Well, I don't know. He's a good swimmer.

PAM. I don't know him.

EILEEN. Neither do I—really.

PAM. Let's go swimming. [*As she and* MARGE *head for the pool,* JEFF *appears and walks over to* EILEEN.]

JEFF. Hi, Eileen.

EILEEN. Hi. It's crowded here today, isn't it?

JEFF. Yeah. [*Several boys and girls are being pushed into the pool. They scream, but they enjoy this. Someone pushes* MARGE *in.* JEFF *turns to* EILEEN.] Marge just got pushed in.

EILEEN. [*Hearing another scream*] And there goes Pam. Sounds like fun.

JEFF. [*Grabbing her*] You're next!. [*He pushes her into the pool. She screams, but she's not fooling around. She is very frightened. When she comes up for air, she opens her mouth to yell. Instead, she swallows some water. She chokes and becomes even more frightened.* JEFF *dives into the pool and tries to help her. Angry and embarrassed, she pushes him away.* MRS. HAYS *comes to the side of the pool and gives a hand to* EILEEN, *who climbs out.* JEFF *follows her. By now, everyone is silent and watching* EILEEN.]

JEFF. Lee, I'm sorry.

EILEEN. [*Embarrassed*] It's okay. I'm okay.

JEFF. I didn't mean to frighten you.

EILEEN. Please, I've got to get out of here!

[*Cut to* MRS. HAYS's *office at the training center for the blind.* JEFF *is with her.*]

MRS. HAYS. It's hard not to make mistakes.

JEFF. But she says she wants to be treated like anybody else.

MRS. HAYS. Yes, but she *isn't* just like everybody else. She's blind. Remember that.

JEFF. Well, it's hard to know where to draw the line. I can try to help her too much, which she hates. Or I can treat her the way I did at the pool. That's bad, too. It seems as if I can't win.

MRS. HAYS. There are some rules that help.

JEFF. Like what?

MRS. HAYS. People without sight don't like being touched without knowing about it first. Suppose a blind person is in a strange room and doesn't know where to sit down. It's best to ask, "May I help you sit down? I'll just take your hand."

JEFF. Yeah, I can see that.

MRS. HAYS. It's not a matter of treating blind people as though they are helpless. It's just being courteous

JEFF. Yeah. She must be really angry with me.

MRS. HAYS. Well, she felt embarrassed as well as frightened. She hates to call attention to herself.

JEFF. It's hard to imagine what it would be like to be blind.

MRS. HAYS. Shut your eyes.

[*He does.*]

And keep them shut.

[*Cut to a taxi cab, which stops in front of* EILEEN's *house.* JEFF *is in the back seat. He is wearing patches over his eyes and dark sunglasses.*]

Words to Know

courteous (KERT ee uhs) *adj.*: Polite and considerate

vendor (VEN der) *n.*: Someone who sells

CAB DRIVER. Here we are.

[JEFF *gets out and walks to the front door of the cab. He feels his way with a cane and his hands.*]

JEFF. How much?

CAB DRIVER. $3.25.

JEFF. Here. [*He holds some bills out. The driver takes four of them and gives* JEFF *some change.*]

CAB DRIVER. Thanks. Can I help you to the house?

JEFF. No, thanks.

[*The cab drives off. Tapping his cane in front of him,* JEFF *moves slowly to the house. He goes up several steps very slowly. He trips over a slight rise in front of the door. He gets up and feels around for the doorbell. He can't find it, so he pounds on the door. Finally, it opens.*]

EILEEN. Who is it?

JEFF. It's me. Jeff.

EILEEN. Why didn't you ring the bell?

JEFF. I couldn't find it.

EILEEN. Why not?

JEFF. I'm blind.

[*Cut to* JEFF *and* EILEEN *walking in the park. He holds her elbow as she guides him.*]

JEFF. So I decided I wanted to know how it feels to be blind. I felt bad about making mistakes with you all the time.

[EILEEN *laughs.*]

What's so funny?

EILEEN. You're talking so loud!

JEFF. [*Loudly*] I am? [*Quietly*] I am?

EILEEN. Yeah. That's one of the tricks of being blind—learning how loud to talk.

JEFF. I never knew that.

EILEEN. [*After a pause*] You can't see a thing?

JEFF. No.

EILEEN. How do you feel?

JEFF. Scared. Every time I take a step, I'm afraid I'll fall a million miles. Do you feel like that?

EILEEN. No. You get over that feeling.

JEFF. How long does it take?

EILEEN. Well, I've been this way all my life. I never knew anything different. It's harder for people who lose their sight.

[*Cut to* EILEEN *and* JEFF *getting hot dogs and sodas at a* vendor's *cart.* JEFF *holds out a handful of coins. The vendor picks out the right amount.* JEFF *and* EILEEN *sit at a table and begin to eat.*]

JEFF. Do people cheat you with money?

EILEEN. No. I always know how much I'm giving.

JEFF. How?

EILEEN. I keep my bills separated with different size paper clips. I use a small clip to hold one-dollar bills, a bigger one for fives, and so on. I can tell coins by feeling. Anyway, I think most people are honest, don't you?

JEFF. I guess so.

[*She laughs.*]

What's so funny?

EILEEN. Where I was trained, they also train sighted people, like Mrs. Hays. They have to go around like you—wearing dark goggles. Once I went out with this sighted man who was wearing goggles. We had lunch, and he asked me to order for both of us. So I ordered spaghetti for him. What a time he had with that stuff. It kept sliding all over the place.

JEFF. You're mean. You know that?

EILEEN. [*Smiling*] Yeah.

[*Cut to them walking toward an outdoor phone booth.*]

JEFF. How do you know your way around so well?

EILEEN. I've been here lots of times. When you're blind, you get maps in your head. The phone booth should be about here. [*She feels it with her cane.*] Excuse me. I promised to call Mom.

JEFF. Okay. [*She goes inside the booth. A small dog runs over to* JEFF *and begins barking. To* JEFF, *the dog sounds huge and dangerous.*] Go away! [*The dog barks louder.*] Leave me alone! [*He pokes out with his cane. The dog snaps at it.* JEFF *gets into the phone booth with* EILEEN.]

EILEEN. [*Into the phone*] Okay, Mom. So long. [*She hangs up and turns to* JEFF.] What's the matter?

JEFF. A wild dog attacked me. He's a monster!

EILEEN. [*Hearing the high-pitched barking moving away*] He sounds pretty small for a monster.

JEFF. I don't care. He's a killer. [*They wait in the booth until the barking has gone away.*]

EILEEN. I guess it's safe now.

JEFF. Yeah, I guess so.

[*Cut to them standing beside a carousel. It is moving. The music is playing.*]

JEFF. Want a ride?

EILEEN. Okay. [*When the carousel stops, they begin to get on. The* TICKET TAKER *sees them and comes over.*]

TICKET TAKER. Hey, you!

JEFF. How much for two?

TICKET TAKER. No way. You'll have to get off.

JEFF. What do you mean?

TICKET TAKER. I can't have blind people on the horses.

JEFF. Why not? I've been on this before.

TICKET TAKER. Not with me here, buddy. I don't have insurance for your kind. Look, I don't want to be mean. [*He takes* JEFF'S *arm.*] Here, I'll help you off.

JEFF. Take your hands off me!

EILEEN. Come on, Jeff. It's okay.

TICKET TAKER. Thanks, lady.

JEFF. It's *not* okay. We're not going to break our necks. We just want a crummy ride, that's all.

EILEEN. Come on, Jeff, please. I'm embarrassed.

JEFF. Okay.

[*Cut to them standing on the curb of a road that runs through the park. They are waiting for the traffic light to change so they can cross the road. They hear a click.*]

EILEEN. Now. Come.

[JEFF *has trouble getting down off the curb.*] Let's go. We don't have much time

[JEFF *moves slowly. He hears the engines of the cars that are waiting. He jumps when he hears a driver rev his engine.* EILEEN *can tell he's very nervous.*]

It's okay. [*They hear another click.*]

JEFF. Did you hear that? [*Cars begin to honk.*] Suppose the cars don't wait.

EILEEN. They will.

[JEFF *panics and begins to rip off his glasses and eye patches.*]

EILEEN. What are you doing?

JEFF. Taking this junk off.

EILEEN. No! [*She takes his arm and leads him to the other curb.*] We're okay. Take it easy.

JEFF. I panicked.

EILEEN. That's natural at first.

JEFF. What a coward I am. How do you do it, Eileen?

EILEEN. You get used to it.

JEFF. Do you *really*?

[*Cut to them walking past some flowers.*]

EILEEN. Wait. [*She leads him to the flowers.*] Smell.

JEFF. They smell good.

EILEEN. Feel. [*They both feel the flowers.*]

JEFF. They're silky.

EILEEN. What kind are they?

JEFF. I don't know.

EILEEN. Do me a favor?

JEFF. Sure.

EILEEN. Take that stuff off your eyes. Then tell me what these flowers are like.

JEFF. Okay. [*He takes off the glasses and eye patches.*] The flowers are yellow. They've got five or six petals each. They're red in the center, with fluffy stuff on them. They're beautiful. [*He looks around.*] Everything is beautiful. The sky. The trees. The grass. Look, Eileen, the colors are fantastic!

EILEEN. [*Sadly*] Yeah.

JEFF. [*Realizing that she can never take off eye patches and see*] I'm sorry.

EILEEN. [*Meaning it*] It's okay. I can feel how nice it is from your voice.

JEFF. [*Staring at her*] You know what's beautiful?

EILEEN. What?

JEFF. You're beautiful.

EILEEN. You mean it?

JEFF. Yes, I mean it.

EILEEN. I believe you.

JEFF. Uh, I heard about this dance our two schools are having. Want to go with me?

EILEEN. Yes, I'd like that.

JEFF. Me, too.
[*Fade out*]

Respond

- What do you think is the most difficult thing about being blind? Why?
- Tell a partner which sense you would be least willing to lose. Why?

Blindness is the total or partial inability to see. Some people are born blind, others may lose their sight through disease or injury. As you discovered in this selection, there are a number of aids that help the visually impaired to read, write, and get around. Many libraries and schools have books in braille or recorded on tape. The Museum of the American Printing House for the Blind, in Kentucky, has exhibits that include historic embossed books, tactile maps and globes, and the first mechanical braillewriters.

Explore Your Reading

Look Back (Recall)

1. How do Jeff and Eileen meet?

Think It Over (Interpret)

2. What is Jeff's real reason for worrying about going to the dance with a girl who is blind?

3. Why does Eileen get angry when people try to help her?

4. How does Jeff react when he covers his eyes for the day? What does this experience teach him about blindness?

Go Beyond (Apply)

5. Do you think Eileen has a kind of "sight" even though she is blind? How would you describe that sight? What does her experience teach you about the way you see the world?

Develop Reading and Literary Skills

Appreciate Stage Directions in Drama

You would have a hard time understanding what happens in "Blind Sunday" if you could not **visualize**—that is, form a mental picture of—the action. **Stage directions**—italicized words in parentheses or brackets that describe characters, setting, and action—make it possible for you to visualize the scenes.

1. How does Jeff discover that Eileen is blind? Which stage directions help you visualize this scene?

2. What two words are used at the beginning of the stage directions that let you know the scene is changing?

3. Describe what happens when Jeff pushes Eileen into the pool, based on what you read in the stage directions. How does this scene help you understand the characters?

Ideas for Writing

In the teleplay, Eileen is able to "see" by using her senses other than sight.

Description Write a paragraph that describes an object without using words that allow readers to use their sense of sight. You can use touch, taste, smell, and sound as well as comparisons. Read your paragraph to classmates and see if they can identify the object.

Journal Entries Write a series of journal entries from Jeff's point of view. These entries should focus on key events in the drama. They can include descriptions of what Jeff saw and felt at these key points in the play.

Ideas for Projects

Relief Map To help a blind student visualize your school, home, or other location, you could create a relief map. Use clay or papier mâché to raise the surface of your map to indicate hallways, classrooms, and other important locations. Use different textures to identify the places.

Community Report Card Inspect your community in terms of how well it accommodates people who are physically challenged. Check parks, schools, playgrounds, libraries, parking lots, malls, and other public areas. If an area receives a low mark, make constructive suggestions for improvement and possibly include them in a letter. Present your findings in an oral report to the class.

How Am I Doing?

Take a moment to respond to these questions in your journal:

Which scenes was I able to visualize most clearly? Why?

What did I learn about how we are different but really the same from reading this teleplay and visualizing its events?

How Are We Different but Really the Same?

Think Critically About the Selections

The selections you have read in this section explore the question "How are we different but really the same?" With a partner or small group, complete one or two of the following activities to show your understanding of the question:

1. Which of the selections taught you something about how you deal with people who are different from you? Explain what you learned and how you learned it. **(Synthesize)**

2. Imagine what it would be like if you were able to introduce a character from one of these selections to a character from another. What would their meeting be like? In what ways would these two characters be different but the same? **(Hypothesize; Draw Conclusions)**

3. Look at the art on this page. Which selection do you think the artist would like best? Why do you think as you do? **(Form and Support a Generalization)**

Student Art *Sale* Rob Nassau
Walt Whitman High School, Bethesda, Maryland

Diversity Poster Create a poster around the idea that we are different but the same. Your poster can be abstract, using colors and shapes to communicate your idea or you can show a scene of cooperation. Put a slogan—that is, a catchy word or phrase—about diversity somewhere on your poster.

Projects

Community Directory Think of the people who share their time, talents, and experience with others to make your community a better place to live. Write an entry for each of these people and organize the entries into a community directory. Present biographical facts as well as background on what the individual has contributed to the community. If possible, include a quotation and a photograph.

Around-the-World Friendship Brochure You have read about friendships among people from locations around the world in this section. In a small group, plan, research, design, and publish a travel brochure of the places you read about. In your brochure, stress the similarities among people in different locations, as well as the unique features of each place. Include photos, magazine pictures, and original artwork in your brochure.

Joining Hands

In this unit, you've been reading and thinking about these important questions:

- **How Do We Care for One Another?**
- **What Are Friends For?**
- **How Are We Different But Really the Same?**

Project Menu

You can find answers to the questions presented in this unit by doing projects on your own or with a group. The answers that come from your participation will stay with you longer than anything anyone can tell you. Here are some ways to join hands and make discoveries together.

Multimedia Presentation on Customs and Relationships No matter what your cultural heritage is or where your family may have come from, relationships always involve sharing among individuals and groups. With a group, do research to find out how these relationships and customs are shown in literature, art, music, and the media in other cultures or from other periods in history. Then create a presentation of your findings using a variety of media. If you want to use this project as part of your portfolio, save your planning notes as well.

Authors and Characters Talk Show As you read the selections in this unit, you explored many different aspects of relationships. With a group, discuss what you think each of the authors or main characters in this unit would say about relationships. Then plan a panel discussion for a talk show about families, friends, and respecting differences, using authors and main characters as "guests." Choose which group members will be guests and which will prepare questions as audience participants. You can perform your talk show live for the rest of the class or videotape it and play it back.

From Questions to Careers

Relationships between people are an important factor in many careers—but especially when the career involves dealing with people on a day–to–day basis. For some people, like Officer Chuck Tsang of the New York City police department, that's the best part of the job. He says:

I always wanted to be a police officer. It gives me the opportunity to talk to the people in the community and make them feel safer.

Officer Tsang knows that establishing good relationships with the people in the community helps a police officer do a good job.

Officers. . . are assigned a beat which they must maintain and be familiar with. Their job on the beat is to go out, get acquainted with the merchants as well as the residents—find out what problems they have—whether they be crime or quality of life problems. You must talk to them and understand their problems.

With a group, brainstorm for a list of other careers that require good "people skills."

Game for Younger Children Brainstorm for strategies that children younger than you can use that will help them get to know and appreciate all the people they might meet. Then, develop a game that children can play in which they gain points for using these and other healthy social skills to show how they appreciate one another for their differences, talents, and experiences. Write a description of the game and its purpose, then create a game board and a set of rules for the game. Make the directions clear and simple enough for children to follow.

Mural Create a collage mural or other display that shows positive relationships among different people in your school or community. Use photos, original art, captions, poems, magazine cut-outs, and other materials to create an interesting design that conveys your message.

Interaction Skits As you read the selections in this unit, you discovered that interacting with other people in a positive way sometimes requires effort and understanding. Often, you must try to imagine what the other person is feeling or experiencing. Choose a relationships problem from one of the selections you have read in this unit. With a group, discuss how you would deal with the problem. Then write a skit incorporating your ideas. Present your skit to the class and lead a follow-up discussion.

Guided Writing

Personal Letter

There are many high-tech ways to communicate these days. It's easier than ever to stay in touch with friends, family members, and acquaintances. Voice mail, E-mail, and cellular phones keep us in close contact. Yet there is still something special about getting a good old ink-on-paper letter in the mail. You can carry the letter with you to reread or to share it with friends. You can save a letter to enjoy again in the future. When is the last time you got a personal letter? When is the last time you wrote one?

Guidelines ●

In writing a personal letter, you

- share news or information with a friend or someone else close to you.

- express your feelings.

- use an informal, conversational tone—make the person receiving the letter feel as if you were right there with him or her.

- use a five-part format that includes a heading, greeting, body of the letter, closing, and signature.

Prewriting

What should I write about?

Write about common interests. Since you're writing to someone you know, write about something that is interesting to both of you. Do you both like the same sport? Do you know a lot of the same people? Bring the person who will receive your letter up-to-date on what's happening in your life.

Jot down your big ideas. Use a scratch pad to remind yourself of what you want or need to say. This will help you keep related thoughts together so your letter will have a logical flow.

Recall the personal letter format. Although a personal letter is an informal piece of writing, there are a few essential things it should have. Letter writers use this format because it's a helpful way of making sure they don't forget something important.

Writing Model

1606 Ivanhoe Lane
Medford, CT 06757
May 12, 1996

> heading

> greeting

Dear Matt,

We did it! We won the championship. . . .

> message

Your dynamic friend,
Raphael

> closing

> signature

Drafting

What are some things I should think about as I write?

Capture your reader's interest. Skip the usual "Hi. How are you?" It's been done! Jump right in with a tidbit of information, a startling statement, or a question. Your reader will keep on reading for curiosity's sake.

Separate different big ideas into their own paragraphs. When you begin to talk about a new topic, make sure you start a new paragraph.

Writing Model

Dear Matt,

Yes! We did it!

> You can tell the writer is excited about something. He uses two exclamations in a row. He also makes his friend guess about what will come next.

Writing Model

. . . so even though we were missing our best goalie (you), we still managed to win. I wish you could have been there!
  So, how's life in sunny California? Have you had a chance to go surfing yet?

> The writer begins a new paragraph when he turns from talking about the soccer playoffs to California and surfing.

Revising and Editing

How can I make my letter more interesting?

Read it out loud. Does it sound the way you and your friend talk to each other? Using contractions usually makes a letter sound more natural and conversational.

Vary your sentence beginnings. Sentences that all begin in the same way sound uninteresting. Look for ways to change sentences around so they begin differently.

Writing Model

Dear Matt,

Yes! We did it! We won the tri-state soccer playoffs, even though we lost our all-time best goalie—you.

> By changing the order of sentence parts, the writer avoided having two sentences begin with *We*.

Check pronoun use. Sometimes deciding which pronoun to use can be confusing. Think about how the pronoun functions in the sentence. Is it a subject or object? Does it show possession? To which previously-used noun does it refer?

Proofread your draft. Are your ideas expressed in a way that makes sense? Have you used correct punctuation and spelling?

> **Computer Tip**
>
> Use the *insert, delete, replace, move, cut,* and *paste* commands as you revise and edit.

Checklist for Revising and Editing • • • • • • • • • • • • • • • • •

- *Where should I start a new paragraph to introduce a new topic?*
- *Which sentence beginnings can I change to add variety?*
- *What pronouns have I used? Which ones need to be changed?*
- *Which part of the letter do I need to add— the heading, greeting, message, closing, or signature?*

 Publishing and Presenting

How can I get a reaction to my letter?

✔ **Mail it.** Address an envelope, put a stamp on it, and send off your letter. Wait for a reply.

✔ **Share it with a classmate.** Talk about things you've done especially well in your letter-writing. Talk, too, about things you might do differently.

How Am I Doing?

Take a moment to answer the following questions:

- *Which notes were most helpful in making my letter flow smoothly?*
- *Which part of my letter did I like best? Why?*

Consider saving a copy of your letter for your portfolio.

Develop Your Style

1 Using Pronouns Correctly

How can I make sure that I use the correct pronoun?

Think how the pronoun works in the sentence. As stand-ins for nouns, pronouns can be used as subjects or objects in a sentence. Here are lists of subject and object pronouns.

Subject Pronouns: Singular: *I, you, he, she, it*
Plural: *we, you, they*
Object Pronouns: Singular: *me, you, him, her, it*
Plural: *us, you, them*

Look back to see what the pronoun is replacing. Make sure you check whether the noun you are replacing is singular or plural.

Practice using pronouns. Identify pronouns that are used incorrectly. Revise those sentences. Some pronouns are used correctly.

1. In June, Rafael and him went to California.
2. The goalie and I celebrated our team's victory.
3. The whole gang and me posed for a team picture.
4. The coach handed the trophy to Jack and me.

Look back at your personal letter. When you talk with someone in person, you don't keep repeating nouns over and over again. Your use of pronouns in your letter makes it sound more conversational. Check to be sure you have used pronouns correctly to stand-in for nouns.

Writing Model

Do you remember when you and ~~me~~ first
learned to play soccer?
                     ^ I

The pronouns *I* and *me* are especially tricky when used with other people. Use the same pronoun you would if you were writing only about yourself. You know that "Remember when I learned to play soccer" is correct and "Remember when me learned to play soccer" is not.

Writing Model

I knew the big guy on the other team would
score a goal. Eventually, ~~they~~ did.
                          ^
                          he

Guy is singular. The pronoun *they* is incorrect because it is plural. The writer was not careful to check which noun—*guy* or *team*—the pronoun was replacing.

2 Vary Sentence Beginnings

How can I keep my sentences from sounding the same?

Be on the lookout for strings of sentences that all begin the same way. If most of your sentences begin with articles, nouns, or pronouns, your writing will be uninteresting and will sound flat. Rewrite some of the sentences so that they have a different beginning or structure.

Use other parts of speech to begin your sentences. Try using verb forms, phrases, and adverbs as sentence starters. Take a look at the differences.

> It will be great to see you on the 8th.
> *Seeing* you on the 8th will be great.

> We can both try when I come to visit next month.
> *When I come to visit next month,* we can both try.

> Those guys from south Jersey usually are fierce.
> *Usually* those guys from south Jersey are fierce.

Practice creating sentence beginnings that have variety. Rewrite sentence beginnings as needed to give the paragraph more variety.

> It is my dream to go to California. I don't think I would have trouble fitting in with kids there. I'd be so far from home, though. I think kids are pretty much the same everywhere. I think that as long as there is music and plenty of pizza I would be happy.

Look at your personal letter. Take a look at the beginnings of your sentences. Do they all begin with an article, noun, or pronoun? Look especially for overuse of the pronoun *I*. Vary some of your sentence beginnings to put a little more personality into your personal letter.

Writing Models

I found a picture of us at our first soccer game. ~~I couldn't believe how~~ *We looked unbelievably young.* ~~young we looked.~~ *When* I showed it to my mother, ~~I think~~ she was surprised, too.

Book News

JOINING

Featured Review

Sounder
by William H. Armstrong

Sounder is the name of a devoted dog owned by an African American family of poor farmers in the South. When the father is arrested for stealing food for his family, Sounder is badly wounded and loses his distinctive bark. The father is sent away to labor camp as punishment, and the dog disappears. The man's son spends years searching for his father and waiting for Sounder's return.

Except for the dog featured in the book, the characters in Sounder have not been identified by names. Places are not named either. This gives the novel a timeless, universal quality. Although the story concerns an African American family, Armstrong has said, "It could have been a poor white family." It is as much a story of poverty, ignorance, and isolation as it is a story of racial conflict.

Sounder is a powerful, moving story about a boy's love, a father's endurance, a dog's devotion, and the painful trials each character undergoes in the search to be reunited with the others.

Introducing the Author

When he was growing up in Virginia, William H. Armstrong had a neighbor who enjoyed telling him stories, including one about a special dog with a unique bark. The novel Sounder is based in part on Armstrong's memory of this tale from his childhood.

Not long after it was written, Sounder was made into a feature film that vividly captures the sights, sounds, and dramatic actions that William Armstrong describes in this classic tale of the South.

Pass It On: Student Choices

Number the Stars by Lois Lowry

Reviewed by Heidi Culp, 6th grade, Eastern Christian Middle School, Wyckoff, New Jersey

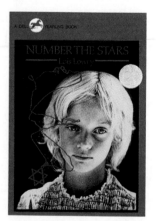

This novel helped me realize how bad things were for some people during World War II. Even though it was set in the past, it has meaning for me today. It showed me that no matter what, you should do all you can to help someone who needs it. The characters were always willing to help one another.

Journal

The Broccoli Tapes
by Jan Slepian

Reviewed by Kristin Wiseman, 6th grade, Glen Park School, New Berlin, Wisconsin

Whenever something good or bad would happen in this novel, I always knew how Sara, the main character, was feeling because of the wonderful descriptions. I liked reading about people who cared for one another, like Grandma and all her relatives, and the kids and Broccoli, the cat. I got so absorbed in this book that I could really feel with the characters and see everything that was happening. I just couldn't put it down.

Walk Two Moons
by Sharon Creech

Reviewed by Vicky Lambino, 6th grade, H. H. Wells School, Brewster, New York

This novel had a lot of messages, like the one that gives the book its title "Don't judge a man 'til you have walked two moons in his moccasins." This book helped me see that all relationships are different, and definitely not always as perfect as people want them to be. I also learned that relationships are

important and valuable. The book is great—but it will probably make you cry. It might even change the way you feel about some of your relationships.

Read On: More Choices

Greening the City Streets: The Story of Community Gardens
by Barbara A. Huff

Science Link

This Same Sky: A Collection of Poems From Around the World
selected by Naomi Shahib Nye

Social Studies Link

Family Pictures Cuadros de familia
by Carmen Lomas Garza

Art Link   Social Studies Link

Share the Fun

Storyboards Draw a series of pictures that represent the major events in a novel you have enjoyed. Make sure your illustrations follow the order of events as they unfold in the book. Display your storyboards for the class.

Response Journal Keep a journal of the thoughts, feelings, and opinions you have about the characters and events in a book you are reading. Jot down ideas about how the story relates to your life. Use your notes as the basis for a group discussion about the book.

Predict the Future With a partner, decide the future of a character in a book you have both read. Support your predictions with information from the story.

GLOSSARY

Pronunciation Key

The vocabulary and footnotes in this textbook are respelled to aid pronunciation. A syllable in CAPITAL LETTERS receives the most stress. The key below lists the letters used for respelling. It includes examples of words using each sound and shows how the words would be respelled.

Symbol	Example	Respelled	Symbol	Example	Respelled
a	hat, cat	hat, cat	oh	no, toe	noh, toh
ay	pay, ape	pay, ayp	oo	look, pull, put	look, pool, poot
ah	hot, stop	haht, stahp	oy	boil, toy	boyl, toy
aw	law, all, horn	law, awl, hawrn	oo	ooze, tool, crew	ooz, tool, croo
			ow	plow, out	plow, owt
e	met, elf, ten	met, elf, ten			
ee	bee, eat, flea	bee, eet, flee	u	up, cut, flood	up, cut, flud
er	learn, sir, fur	lern, ser, fer	yoo	few, use	fyoo, yooz
i	is	fit	uh	a in ago	uh GO
ī	mile, sigh	mīle sīgh		e in agent	AY juhnt
				i in sanity	SAN uh tee
				o in compress	kuhm PRES
				u in focus	FOH kuhs

A

abruptly (uh BRUPT lee) *adv*.: Suddenly; unexpectedly

Abuelita (ah bwel EET uh) *n*.: Affectionalte name for grandmother

alter (AWL ter) *v*.: Change; become different

apprentice (uh PREN tis) *n*.: A person who agrees to work for a craftsman for a certain amount of time in exchange for instruction in the craft

authentic (aw THEN tik) *adj*.: Real and believable

B

bloat (BLOHT) *v*.: Puff and swell

bore (BAWR) *v*.: Make a hole or tunnel

bound (BOWND) *v*.: Tied

braille (BRAYL) *n*.: A system of reading and writing in which letters and numbers are shown by patterns of raised dots that can be felt

C

confide (cahn FĪD) *v*.: Share a private thought or idea

convert (cahn VERT) *v*.: Change

cordial (KOR juhl) *adv*.: In a friendly way

corridor (CAWR i dawr) *n*.: A long passageway or hallway

courteous (KERT ee uhs) *adj*.: Polite and considerate

crepe (KRAYP) *n*.: Thin, crinkled cloth

D

deftly (DEFT lee) *adv*.: Skillfully and easily

dense (DENS) *adj*.: Very thick

devastate (DEV uhs tayt) *adj*.: Overwhelm; destroy

devise (di VĪZ) *v*.: Work out by thinking

discriminate (dis KRIM i nayt) *v*.: Treat one group differently from another

dreidel (DRAY duhl) *n*.: A game played with a top during Hanukkah

E

eddy (ED dee) *n*.: Little whirlwind

emigrate (EM i grayt) *v*.: Leave one country to settle in another

end (END) *n*.: Purpose or goal

exquisite (eks KWIZ it) *adj*.: Very beautifully done; of very high quality

exude (eg ZOOD) *v*.: Pour out

F

fluently (FLOO int lee) *adv*.: Easily, smoothly

frequently (FREE kwuhnt lee) *adv*.: Often; many times

frolic (FRAHL ik) *v*.: Play or romp about

furtively (FER tiv lee) *adv*.: In a hidden way

G

gladiator (GLAD ee ay ter) *n*.: In ancient Rome, the men who fought against other men or against wild animals for the entertainment of the crowds

grope (GROHP) *v*.: Search about blindly by feeling the way

gulden (GOOL den) *n*.: Unit of money

H

Hanukkah (HAH noo kah) *n*.: The Jewish "Festival of Lights," usually celebrated during December

hideous (HID ee uhs) *adj*.: Horrible; dreadfully frightening

hob (HAHB) *n*.: A little ledge at the back of the fireplace for keeping a kettle or saucepan warm

Holocaust (HAHL uh kahst) *n*.: The Nazi's systematic destruction of more than six million European Jews before and during World War II

horizontally (hahr i ZAHNT uh lee) *adv*.: From one side to the other

humbly (HUHMB lee) *adj*.: Without pride; with respect to the person of higher rank

I

incessantly (in SES uhnt lee) *adv*.: Without stopping

incredulous (in KREJ yoo luhs) *adj*.: Unwilling or unable to believe

insightful (in SĪT fuhl) *adj*.: Having the ability to see more than the surface; to understand the inner meaning

instinctively (in STINK tiv lee) *adv*.: Naturally; without needing to think

intersection (IN ter sek shuhn) *n*.: Place where two or more roads cross one another

intimacy (IN tuh muh see) *n*.: A very personal closeness

J

jar (JAHR) *v*.: Jolt or shake

L

lair (LAYR) *n*.: The den, or resting place, of a wild animal

level (LEV uhl) *v*.: Flatten; demolish

locks (LAHKS) *n*.: Hair

M

meager (MEE ger) *adj*.: Poor; very little

minuscule (MI nuhs kyool) *adj*.: Very small; tiny

moor (MOOR) *n*.: Wide open field of marshy land

N

neglect (ni GLEKT) *v*.: Not care for; ignore

nugget (NUHG it) *n*.: Lump

P

paddy (PAD dee) *n*.: A rice field

peddler (PED ler) *n*.: A person who walked from town to town selling things

peninsula (puh NIN suh luh) *n*.: An area of land almost entirely surrounded by water

persecution (per suh KYOO shuhn) *n*.: Cruel and unfair treatment, often because of politics, religion, or race

phonograph (FOHN uh grahf) *n*.: Record player

piqué (pee KAY) *n*.: Cotton cloth with ridges like corduroy

placid (PLAHS id) *adj*.: Calm and peaceful

precious (PRESH uhs) *adj*.: Beloved

profit (PRAHF it) *v*.: Give an advantage to

Q

quetzal (ket SAHL) *n*.: A crested bird of Central America, usually bright green above and red below, with long streaming tail feathers

R

range (RANJ) *n*.: Wide assortment

ranging (RANJ ing) *v*.: Wandering about; roaming

rapidly (RAHP id lee) *adv*.: Very quickly

refugee (ref yoo JEE) *n*.: A person who has run from his or her home or country to escape war

resemble (ree SEM buhl) *v*.: Look like

resin (REZ in) *n*.: A sticky substance, like sap, that oozes from some plants and trees

retort (ree TAWRT) *v*.: Reply sharply

S

sage (SAYJ) *n*.: A very wise person

seldom (SEL duhm) *adv*.: Rarely

shed (SHED) *v*.: Throw off

shilling (SHIL ing) *n*.: A British coin, not used anymore. It was worth about 12 cents

ship's hold (SHIPS hohld) *n*.: The inside of the ship, under the decks, where cargo is usually carried

slender (SLEN der) *adj*.: Thin

solitude (SAHL uh tood) *n*.: The condition of being alone

sonar (SOH nahr) *n*.: Stands for **s**ound **n**avigation **a**nd **r**anging; objects are located by sending out high frequency sound waves and measuring the vibrations that are bounced back

sovereign (SAHV rin) *adj*.: Supreme; ruling above all others

stingiest (STIN jee est) *adj*.: The most unwilling to spend any money; miserly

suet (SOO it) *n*.: The fatty part of meat

supple (SUHP uhl) *adj*.: Able to bend and move easily

suppress (suh PRES) *v*.: Force back or squash down

T

thicket (THIK it) *n*.: A bunch of bushes and small trees

tortilla (tor TEE yuh) *n*.: Very thin, flat, round cake made of corn meal or flour

traje (TRAH hay) *n*.: Traditional clothing

V

vacant (VAY kint) *adj*.: Empty

vaguely (VAYG lee) *adv*.: In a hazy, uncertain way

variation (vahr ee AY shuhn) *n*.: A slightly different form

vendor (VEN der) *n*.: Someone who sells

vertically (VER tik lee) *adv*.: From top to bottom or bottom to top

W

warily (WAYR uh lee) *adv*.: Carefully and cautiously

wracked (RAKT) *adj*.: Overcome with great suffering

Y

youth (YOOTH) *n*.: A young person

Index of Fine Art

Index of Authors and Titles

Page numbers in italics refer to biographical information.

Index of Skills

Student Review Board

Acharya, Arundhathi
Cecelia Snyder Middle School
Bensalem, Pennsylvania

Adkisson, Grant
McClintock Middle School
Charlotte, North Carolina

Akuna, Kimberly
Harriet Eddy Middle School
Elk Grove, California

Amdur, Samantha
Morgan Selvidge Middle School
Ballwin, Missouri

Arcilla, Richard
Village School
Closter, New Jersey

Arredondo, Marcus
Keystone School
San Antonio, Texas

Auten, Kristen
Bernardo Heights Middle School
San Diego, California

Backs, Jamie
Cross Keys Middle School
Florissant, Missouri

Baldwin, Katie
Bonham Middle School
Temple, Texas

Barber, Joanna
Chenery School
Belmont, Massachusetts

Bates, Maureen
Chestnut Ridge Middle School
Sewell, New Jersey

Bates, Meghan
Chestnut Ridge Middle School
Sewell, New Jersey

Beber, Nick
Summit Middle School
Dillon, Colorado

Becker, Jason
Hicksville Middle School
Hicksville, New York

Belfon, Loreal
Highland Oaks Middle School
Miami, Florida

Belknap, Jessica
Hughes Middle School
Long Beach, California

Bennet, Joseph
Conner Middle School
Hebron, Kentucky

Birke, Lori
LaSalle Springs Middle School
Glencoe, Missouri

Bleichrodt, Angela
Beulah School
Beulah, Colorado

Block, Kyle
Hall-McCarter Middle School
Blue Springs, Missouri

Brendecke, Sarah Grant
Baseline Middle School
Boulder, Colorado

Brooks, Beau
Cresthill Middle School
Highlands Ranch, Colorado

Bruder, Jennifer
Nipher Middle School
Kirkwood, Missouri

Brunsfeld, Courtney
Moscow Junior High School
Moscow, Idaho

Burnett, Joseph
Markham Intermediate School
Placerville, California

Burrows, Tammy
Meadowbrook Middle School
Orlando, Florida

Calles, Miguel
Lennox Middle School
Lennox, California

Casanova, Christina
McKinley Classic Junior Academy
St. Louis, Missouri

Ceaser, Cerena
Templeton Middle School
Templeton, California

Chapman, Jon
Black Butte Middle School
Shingletown, California

Cho, Hwa
Miami Lakes Middle School
Miami Lakes, Florida

Chu, Rita
Orange Grove Middle School
Hacienda Heights, California

Church, John
Nathan Hale Middle School
Norwalk, Conneticut

Clouse, Melissa Ann
Happy Valley Elementary School
Anderson, California

Colbert, Ryanne
William H. Crocker School
Hillsborough, California

Crucet, Jennine
Miami Lakes Middle School
Miami Lakes, Florida

Culp, Heidi
Eastern Christian Middle School
Wyckoff, New Jersey

Cummings, Amber
Pacheco Elementary School
Redding, California

Curran, Christopher
Cresthill Middle School
Highlands Ranch, Colorado

D'Angelo, Samantha
Cresthill Middle School
Highlands Ranch, Colorado

D'Auria, Jeffrey
Nyack Middle School
Nyack, New York

D'Auria, Katherine
Upper Nyack Elementary School
Upper Nyack, New York

D'Auria, Patrick
Nyack Middle School
Nyack, New York

Daughtride, Katharyne
Lakeview Middle School
Winter Garden, Florida

Donato, Bridget
Felix Festa Junior High School
New City, New York

Donato, Christopher
Felix Festa Junior High School
New City, New York

Dress, Brian
Hall-McCarter Middle School
Blue Springs, Missouri

Drilling, Sarah
Milford Junior High School
Milford, Ohio

Fernandez, Adrian
Shenandoah Middle School
Coral Gables, Florida

Flores, Amanda
Orange Grove Middle School
Hacienda Heights, California

Flynn, Patricia
Camp Creek Middle School
College Park, Georgia

Ford, Adam
Cresthill Middle School
Highlands Ranch, Colorado

Fowler, Sabrina
Camp Creek Middle School
College Park, Georgia

Fox, Anna
Georgetown School
Georgetown, California

Freeman, Ledon
Atlanta, Georgia

Frid-Nielsen, Snorre
Branciforte Elementary School
Santa Cruz, California

Frosh, Nicole
Columbia Middle School
Aurora, Colorado

Gerretson, Bryan
Marshfield Junior High School
Marshfield, Wisconsin

Gillis, Shalon Michelle
Wagner Middle School
Philadelphia, Pennsylvania

Gonzales, Michael
Kitty Hawk Junior High School
Universal City, Texas

Goodman, Andrew
Richmond School
Hanover, New Hampshire

Granberry, Kemoria
Riviera Middle School
Miami, Florida

Groppe, Karissa
McCormic Junior High School
Cheyenne, Wyoming

Hadley, Michelle
Hopkinton Middle School
Hopkinton, Massachusetts

Hall, Katie
C.R. Anderson Middle School
Helena, Montana

Hamilton, Tim
Columbia School
Redding, California

Hawkins, Arie
East Norriton Middle School
Norristown, Pennsylvania

Hawkins, Jerry
Carrollton Junior High School
Carrollton, Missouri

Hayes, Bridget
Point Fermin Elementary School
San Pedro, California

Heinen, Jonathan
Broomfield Heights Middle School
Broomfield, Colorado

Hibbard, Erin
Willard Grade Center
Ada, Oklahoma

Hinners, Katie
Spaulding Middle School
Loveland, Ohio

Houston, Robert
Allamuchy Township Elementary
Allamuchy, New Jersey

Huang, Kane
Selridge Middle School
Ballwin, Missouri

Hudson, Vanessa
Bates Academy
Detroit, Michigan

Hutchison, Erika
C.R. Anderson Middle School
Helena, Montana

Hykes, Melissa
Meadowbrook Middle School
Orlando, Florida

Jackson, Sarah Jane
Needles Middle School
Needles, California

Jigarjian, Kathryn
Weston Middle School
Weston, Massachusetts

Johnson, Becky
Wheatland Junior High School
Wheatland, Wyoming

Johnson, Bonnie
West Middle School
Colorado Springs, Colorado

Johnson, Courtney
Oak Run Elementary School
Oak Run, California

Jones, Mary Clara
Beulah Middle School
Beulah, Colorado

Jones, Neil
Central School
Chillicothe, Missouri

Juarez, Sandra
Adams City Middle School
Thornton, Colorado

Juarez, Karen
Rincon Middle School
Escondito, California

Karas, Eleni
Our Lady of Grace
Encino, California

King, Autumn
Roberts Paideia Academy
Cincinnati, Ohio

Kossenko, Anna
Plantation Middle School
Plantation, Florida

Kurtz, Rachel
Paul Revere Middle School
Los Angeles, California

Lambino, Victoria
Henry H. Wells Middle School
Brewster, New York

Lamour, Katleen
Highland Oaks Middle School
North Miami Beach, Florida

Larson, Veronica
McClintock Middle School
Charlotte, North Carolina

Liao, Wei-Cheng
Nobel Middle School
Northridge, California

Lightfoot, Michael
Mission Hill Middle School
Santa Cruz, California

Lippman, Andrew
Thomas A. Blake Middle School
Medfield, Massachusetts

Lo, Melissa
Lincoln Middle School
Santa Monica, California

Lopez, Eric
Irvine Intermediate School
Costa Mesa, California

Lowery, Ry-Yon
East Norriton Middle School
Norristown, Pennsylvania

Macias, Edgar
Teresa Hughes Elementary School
Cudahy, California

Madero, Vanessa
Mathew J. Brletic Elementary
Parlier, California

Mandel, Lily
Mission Hill Junior High School
Santa Cruz, California

Manzano, Elizabeth Josephine
Hillside Elementary School
San Bernardino, California

Marentes, Crystal-Rose
Orange Grove Middle School
Hacienda Heights, California

Martinez, Desiree
Wheatland Junior High School
Wheatland, Wyoming

Massey, Drew
Union 6th and 7th Grade Center
Tulsa, Oklahoma

Matson, Josh
Canyon View Junior High School
Orem, Utah

Maxcy, Donald, Jr.
Camp Creek Middle School
Atlanta, Georgia

Maybruch, Robyn
Middle School 141
Riverdale, New York

Mayer, Judith
Burlingame Intermediate School
Burlingame, California

McCarter, Jennifer
Washburn School
Cincinnati, Ohio

McCarthy, Megan
Richmond School
Hanover, New Hampshire

McCombs, Juanetta
Washburn School
Cincinnati, Ohio

McGann, Kristen
Orange Grove Middle School
Hacienda Heights, California

McKelvey, Steven
Providence Christian Academy
Atlanta, Georgia

McQuary, Megan
CCA Baldi Middle School
Philadelphia, Pennsylvania

Mercier, Jared
Marshfield Junior High School
Marshfield, Wisconsin

Merrill, Nick
Windham Middle School
Windham, Maine

Miller, Catherine
Neil Armstrong Junior High School
Levittown, Pennsylvania

Miller, Kristen
Marina Village Junior High
El Dorado Hills, California

Montgomery, Tyler
North Cow Creek School
Palo Cedro, California

Mueller, Jessica
Spaulding Middle School
Loveland, Ohio

Mueler, John
St. Catherine School
Milwaukee, Wisconsin

Mulligan, Rebecca
Herbert Hoover Middle School
Oklahoma City, Oklahoma

Murgel, John
Beulah School
Beulah, Colorado

Murphy, Mathew
St. Wenceslaus School
Omaha, Nebraska

Neeley, Alex
Allamuchy Township School
Allamuchy, New Jersey

Nelsen-Smith, Nicole Marie
Branciforte Elementary
Santa Cruz, California

Ogle, Sarah
Redlands Middle School
Grand Junction, Colorado

Ozeryansky, Svetlana
C.C.A. Baldi Middle School
Philadelphia, Pennsylvania

Pacheco, Vicky
East Whittier Middle School
Whittier, California

Paddack, Geoffrey
Ada Junior High School
Ada, Oklahoma

Palombi, Stephanie
Marina Village Middle School
Cameron Park, California

Panion, Stephanie
Pitts Middle School
Pueblo, Colorado

Parks, Danny
West Cottonwood Junior High School
Cottonwood, California

Parriot, Cassandra
Orange Grove Middle School
Hacienda Heights, California

Paulson, Christina
Jefferson Middle School
Rocky Ford, Colorado

Perez, Iscura
Charles Drew Middle School
Los Angeles, California

Pratt, Lisa
Nottingham Middle Community Education Center
St. Louis, Missouri

Raggio, Jeremiah
Eagleview Middle School
Colorado Springs, Colorado

Raines, Angela
McKinley Classical Academy
St. Louis, Missouri

Ramadan, Mohammad
Ada Junior High School
Ada, Oklahoma

Ramiro, Leah
Magruder Middle School
Torrance, California

Raymond, Elizabeth
Julia A. Traphagen School
Waldwick, New Jersey

Recinos, Julie
Riviera Middle School
Miami, Florida

Reese, Andrea
Moscow Junior High
Moscow, Idaho

Reiners, Andrew
Redlands Middle School
Grand Junction, Colorado

Riddle, Katy
Willard Elementary School
Ada, Oklahoma

Rippe, Chris
La Mesa Junior High School
Santa Clarita, California

Robinson, Barbara
Wagner Middle School
Philadelphia, Pennsylvania

Rochford, Tracy
Louis Armstrong Middle School/IS 227
East Elmhurst, New York

Rodriguez, Ashley
John C. Martinez Junior High School
Parlier, California

Rowe, Michael
Washington Middle School
Long Beach, California

Sayles, Nichole
Hall McCarter Middle School
Blue Springs, Missouri

Schall, Harvest
Castle Rock Elementary School
Castella, California

Schellenberg, Katie
Corpus Christi School
Pacific Palisades, California

Schmees, Katherine
Milford Junior High School
Milford, Ohio

Schned, Paul
Richmond School
Hanover, New Hampshire

Schneider, Jennie
Parkway West Middle School
Chesterfield, Missouri

Scialanga, Michelle
Taylor Middle School
Millbrae, California

Shye, Kathryn
Happy Valley Elementary School
Anderson, California

Sirikulvadhana, Tiffany
Orange Grove Middle School
Hacienda Heights, California

Smetak, Laura
Orange Grove Middle School
Hacienda Heights, California

Smith, Shannon
Mary Putnam Henck Intermediate School
Lake Arrowhead, California

Smith-Paden, Patricia
Chappelow Middle School
Evans, Colorado

Sones, Mandy
Knox Junior High School
The Woodlands, Texas

Song, Sarah
Orange Grove Middle School
Hacienda Heights, California

Souza, Molly
Georgetown School
Georgetown, California

Stewart, Larry
Windsor Elementary School
Cincinnati, Ohio

Stites, Aaron
Redlands Middle School
Grand Junction, Colorado

Sturzione, James Van Duyn
Glen Rock Middle School
Glen Rock, New Jersey

Sundberg, Sarah
Milford Junior High School
Milford, Ohio

Swan, Tessa
Pacheco Elementary School
Redding, California

Swanson, Kurt
Allamuchy Elementary School
Allamuchy, New Jersey

Swihart, Bruce
Redlands Middle School
Grand Junction, Colorado

Syron, Christine
Nottingham Middle Community Education Center
St. Louis, Missouri

Taylor, Cody
Bella Vista Elementary School
Bella Vista, California

Thomas, Jennifer
Hoover Middle School
San Jose, California

Thompson, Robbie
Hefner Middle School
Oklahoma City, Oklahoma

Todd, Wanda
Hampton Middle School
Detroit, Michigan

Torning, Fraser
Allamuchy Elementary School
Allamuchy, New Jersey

Torres, Erica
Truman Middle School
Albuquerque, New Mexico

Tyroch, Melissa
Bonham Middle School
Temple, Texas

Ulibarri, Shavonne
John C. Martinez Junior High School
Parlier, California

Vanderham, Lynsey
Eagleview Middle School
Colorado Springs, Colorado

Vemula, Suni
Ada Junior High School
Ada, Oklahoma

Venable, Virginia
Chillicothe Junior High School
Chillicothe, Missouri

Vickers, Lori
Lake Braddock Secondary School
Springfield, Virginia

Vickers, Vanessa
Kings Glen School
Springfield, Virginia

Villanueva, Rene
John C. Martinez Junior High School
Parlier, California

Villasenor, Jose
Dana Middle School
San Pedro, California

Ward, Kimberly
Desert Horizon Elementary School
Phoenix, Arizona

Weeks, Josanna
Bellmont Middle School
Decatur, Indiana

West, Tyrel
Wheatland Junior High School
Wheatland, Wyoming

Whipple, Mike
Canandaigua Middle School
Canandaigua, New York

White, Schaefer
Richmond Middle School
Hanover, New Hampshire

Wilhelm, Paula
Wheatland Junior High School
Wheatland, Wyoming

Williams, Bonnie
Washburn School
Cincinnati, Ohio

Williams, Jason
Parkway West Middle School
Chesterfield, Missouri

Wiseman, Kristin
Glen Park Elementary School
New Berlin, Wisconsin

Wiseman, Megan
Glen Park Elementary School
New Berlin, Wisconsin

Yu, Veronica
Piñon Mesa Middle School
Victorville, California

Zipse, Elizabeth
Redlands Middle School
Grand Junction, Colorado

Acknowledgments (continued)

Dial Books for Young Readers, a division of Penguin Books USA Inc.
"A Fluent Friendship" from *Going Home* by Nicholasa Mohr. Copyright © 1986 by Nicholasa Mohr. Used by permission of Dial Books for Young Readers, a division of Penguin Books USA Inc.

Dramatic Publishing
Excerpt from *I Saved a Winter Just For You*, adapted by Tom Erhard. Copyright © 1984 by Thomas A. Erhard. Excerpt from *Inside Out-Upside Down* by Karen Groene, Maggie Mudd, Susan MacDonnell, and Will Oldham. Copyright © 1986 by Walden Theatre, Nancy Sexton, Director. All rights reserved. All inquiries regarding performance rights should be addressed to Dramatic Publishing Company, 311 Washington Street, Woodstock, IL 60098. Reprinted by permission of Dramatic Publishing.

Franklin Watts, Inc., a division of Grolier Incorporated
"Anna" from *New Kids On the Block: Oral Histories of Immigrant Teens* by Janet Bode. Copyright © 1989 by Janet Bode. All rights reserved. Reprinted by permission of Franklin Watts, Inc., a division of Grolier Incorporated.

Free To Be Foundation, Inc.
"The Biggest Problem (Is in Other People's Minds)," words and music by Don Haynie, published in *Free To Be Family* conceived by Marlo Thomas. Copyright © 1987 by Free To Be Foundation, Inc.

Georgia Gelmis
"In Teaching a Friend to Fly" by Georgia Gelmis, published in Saint Ann's Middle School Literary Magazine 1992-1993. Reprinted by permission of the author.

Greenwillow Books, a division of William Morrow & Company, Inc.
"Door Number Four" from *If I Had A Paka* by Charlotte Pomerantz. Copyright © 1982 by Charlotte Pomerantz. Reprinted by permission of Greenwillow Books, a division of William Morrow & Company, Inc.

Harcourt Brace & Company
"Blintzes Stuffed with Cheese: Isaac Bashevis Singer" from *Lives of the Writers: Comedies, Tragedies (and What the Neighbors Thought)*, copyright © 1994 by Kathleen Krull. Reprinted by permission of Harcourt Brace & Company.

HarperCollins Publishers
"The Little Boy and the Old Man" from *A Light in the Attic* by Shel Silverstein. Copyright © 1981 by Evil Eye Music, Inc. "Zlateh the Goat" from *Zlateh the Goat and Other Stories* by Isaac Bashevis Singer. "Friendship" from *Brown Angels: an Album of Pictures and Verse* by Walter Dean Myers. "My Best Friend" by Lessie Little Jones, from *Childtimes: A Three-Generation Memoir* by Eloise Greenfield. Copyright © 1979 by Eloise Greenfield and Lessie Jones Little. Reprinted by permission of HarperCollins Publishers.

Alfred A. Knopf, Inc.
"He Lion, Bruh Bear and Bruh Rabbit" from *The People Could Fly* by Virginia Hamilton. Text copyright © 1985 by Virginia Hamilton. Reprinted by permission of Alfred A. Knopf, Inc.

Lee & Low Books, Inc.
Bein With You This Way by W. Nikola-Lisa. Text copyright © 1994 by W. Nikola-Lisa. Reproduced with permission of Lee & Low Books Inc., New York.

Many Cultures Publishing
The Mountain of the Men & the Mountain of the Women , as told by Touch Neak, translated by Samol Tan and written by Alice Lucas. Published by Many Cultures Publishing from the *Voices of Liberty Series*. Reprinted by permission of the publisher.

Museum of New Mexico Press
"The Boy and His Grandfather" is reprinted with permission of the Museum of New Mexico Press from *Cuentos: Tales from the Hispanic Southwest* by José Griego y Maestas and Rudolfo Anaya, copyright © 1980.

Simon J. Ortiz
"A Story of How a Wall Stands" by Simon J. Ortiz, from *Woven Stone*, University of Arizona Press, Tucson, AZ 1992. Reprinted by permission of the author.

Deborah Paley, for the author
"Listening" by Laura Paley, from *St. Ann's Middle School Literary Magazine*, 1991-1992. Reprinted by permission of Deborah Paley for the author.

Putnam Publishing Group
"The Haste-Me-Well Quilt" by Elizabeth Yates is reprinted by permission from *Under the Little Fir* by Elizabeth Yates. Copyright © 1942 by Coward-McCann, Inc.

Simon & Schuster Books for Young Readers
"The Friends of Kwan Ming" from *Tales from Gold Mountain: Stories of the Chinese in the New World* by Paul Yee. Text copyright © 1989 by Paul Yee. Reprinted by permission of Simon & Schuster Books for Young Readers.

Scott Treimel New York
"People" from *All That Sunlight* by Charlotte Zolotow. Text copyright © 1967 by Charlotte Zolotow. Reprinted by permission of Scott Treimel New York.

Daniel Wilson Productions, Inc.
"Blind Sunday," adapted from the television script *Blind Sunday* by Arthur Barron. © 1976 Daniel Wilson Productions, Inc. Used by permissiion of Daniel Wilson Productions, Inc.
Note: Every effort has been made to locate the copyright owner of material reprinted in this book. Omissions brought to our attention will be corrected in subsequent printings.

Photo and Fine Arts Credits

Boldface numbers refer to the page on which the art is found.

Cover: Untitled, Margaret Noel, Walt Whitman High School, Bethesda, Maryland **Bv:** *Family Photos*, Hila Sela, Artwork from the permanent collection of THIRTEEN/WNET's Student Arts Festival, 1978–1993; **Bvi:** Untitled, Courtney Denham, Natalie Garrett, Linette Cheng, Che Chen, Paul Maylone, Michele Miller, Glen Kessler, Pat Daughters, Ben Shupe, Walt Whitman High School, Bethesda, Maryland; **Bvii:** *"Sale,"* Rob Nassau, Walt Whitman High School, Bethesda, Maryland; **Bviii:** (background) Prentice Hall; (bottom) Courtesy of the artist; **Bix:** Prentice Hall; **Bx:** Courtesy of the artist; **B4:** (left) Harald Sund/Image Bank; **B5:** (top) Jack Baker/Image Bank; (bottom) The Bettmann Archive; **B7:** *Family Photos*, Hila Sela, Artwork from the permanent collection of THIRTEEN/WNET's Student Arts Festival, 1978–1993; **B8:** (left) *Sharing America, 1990* (detail of quilt) Little Stitch Makers, LaCrosse WI, Photograph Courtesy of the Museum of American Folk Art; **B9:** (right) *America Discovered Through Quilts: Past, Present and Future, 1990,* Jean A. Natrop, Photograph Courtesy of the Museum of American Folk Art; **B10:** *Discover America One Patch at a Time, 1990,* (detail) Joyce Winterton Stewart, Rexburg Idaho, Photograph Courtesy of the Museum of American Folk Art; **B11:** *Friends Sharing America,* 1990, Three Friends, Clinton MI, Photograph Courtesy of the Museum of American Folk Art; **B12:** *Memories Playground, 1988,* Sheila Ruth Maloney, Zephyr, Ontario, Canada, Photograph Courtesy of the Museum of American Folk Art; **B14:** New York Times Pictures; **B16–17:** (background) Prentice Hall; **B17:** (bottom) Courtesy of the artist; **B18:** (bottom) Prentice Hall; **B18–19:** (background) Prentice Hall; **B20:** Geoff Goslon/Image Bank; **B22:** (left) Culver Pictures, Inc.; (right) Michael Ochs Archives, **B24:** (right) Mireille Vautier /Woodfin Camp & Associates; **B26:** (bottom) *"Las Companeras De Chichicastenango"* 1992, Donna Clair, oil/Belgian linen, 36"x48" © Donna Clair 1992, Taos NM. All rights reserved.; **B27:** (right) David Young-Wolff/Photo Edit; **B28:** (left) Jean-Gérard Sidaner/Photo Researchers, Inc.; **B29:** (tr) Charles Mason; **B31:** *Family Photos*, Hila Sela, Artwork from the permanent collection of THIRTEEN/WNET's Student Arts Festival, 1978–1993; **B33:** Salt Lake Tribune, photo by Lynn Johnson; **B36:** (bottom) Harcourt Brace & Company, Photo by Paul Brewer, **B38:** (right) Courtesy of the artist; **B40:** Courtesy of the artist; **B41:** (right) Eloise

Greenfield, photo by David Jones; **B43:** Untitled, Courtney Denham, Natalie Garrett, Linette Cheng, Che Chen, Paul Maylone, Michele Miller, Glen Kessler, Pat Daughters, Ben Shupe, Walt Whitman High School, Bethesda, Maryland; **B46, B47, B49:** from "Zlateh the Goat and Other Stories" by Isaac Bashevis Singer, illustrations by Maurice Sendak, Harper & Row, Publishers, Inc.; **B50:** The Granger Collection, New York; **B52:** Jeanne White Photo/Photo Researchers, Inc.; **B53:** (left) Courtesy of the author, photo by Debbie Paley; (center) Renee Lynn/Photo Researchers, Inc.; **B54:** (top) *Busy in Paradise, 1984,* oil on canvas 88"x138" Derek Boshier, Texas Gallery, Houston; (bottom) Courtesy of the author; **B56, B57:** Grace Davies/Omni-Photo Communications, Inc.; **B62:** Shadowplay Press; **B64:** Culver Pictures, Inc.; **B65:** Reprinted with the permission of Simon & Schuster for Young Readers, an imprint of Simon & Schuster Children's Publishing Division from TALES FROM GOLD MOUNTAIN by Paul Yee, paintings by Simon Ng. Illustration copyright (c) 1989 Simon Ng.; **B67:** Courtesy, The Bancroft Library; **B68:** Groundwood/Douglas & McIntyre Children's Books; **B69:** (top) Vera Bradshaw /Photo Researchers, Inc.; (bottom) David Burckhalter Photography; **B71:** Untitled, Courtney Denham, Natalie Garrett, Linette Cheng, Che Chen, Paul Maylone, Michele Miller, Glen Kessler, Pat Daughters, Ben Shupe, Walt Whitman High School, Bethesda, Maryland; **B73:** Prentice Hall; **B74–75:** (background) Romilly Lockyer/Image Bank; **B75:** (background) G.R.Roberts/Omni-Photo Communications, Inc.; (center) *Striding Grizzly, 1989,* Ken Bunn, Bronze 52 x 20 x 29 ¹/₂, National Museum of Wildlife Art, Jackson, Wyoming; **B76:** (background) G.R.Roberts/Omni-Photo Communications, Inc.; (bl) Courtesy of the artist; **B77:** (background) G.R.Roberts/Omni-Photo Communications, Inc.; (top) *Lola,* Rabbit in bronze, Dan Ostermiller, Claggett/Rey Gallery, Vail, Colorado; **B78:** (background) G.R.Roberts/ Omni-Photo Communications, Inc.; (right) Prentice Hall; **B79:** (background) G.R.Roberts/Omni-Photo Communications, Inc.; **B80–81:** (background) Mike Yamashita/Woodfin Camp & Associates; **B82–83:** (background) Vivian M. Peevers/Peter Arnold, Inc.; **B84–85:** (background) Mike Yamashita/ Woodfin Camp & Associates; **B87:** *"Sale,"* Rob Nassau, Walt Whitman High School, Bethesda, Maryland; **B88:** Gerhard Gscheidle/Peter Arnold, Inc.; **B89:** Dinodia/Omni-Photo Communications, Inc.; **B90:** (top) David Young-Wolff/Photo Edit; (bottom) Courtesy of the author; **B91:** (top) & (bottom) Lawrence Migdale Photography; **B92–93:** Courtesy of the artist; **B94:** (top) Lawrence Migdale Photography; (bottom) Lee & Low Books, Inc.; **B97:** Richard Barnett/Omni-Photo Communications, Inc.; **B98:** Erika Stone/Peter Arnold, Inc.; **B99:** Erich Lessing/Art Resource/NY; **B100:** Courtesy of Paintbrush Diplomacy; **B101:** Nimatallah/Art Resource,NY; **B102:** Courtesy of the author, Photo by Stan Mack; **B104–105, B107:** Photo by Silver Burdett Ginn; **B108:** Arte Publico Press. Photo by Phil Cantor; **B110–111:** *One Child Between Doors (Seorang Anak di Antara Pintu Ruang) 1984,* Dede Eri Supria, oil on canvas, 139x160cm, Courtesy of Joseph Fischer; **B112:** (top) *The Marble Players,* Stephen Scott Young, watercolor on paper 22"x30" Photography courtesy of John H. Surovek Gallery, Palm Beach, Florida; (center) John Craig Photo; (bottom) Hearst Books, Photo by Daniel Pomerantz; **B127:** *"Sale,"* Rob Nassau, Walt Whitman High School, Bethesda, Maryland; **B129:** Prentice Hall; **B131:** Patrick Vielcanet/Photo Researchers, Inc.; **B136:** (left) Full cover of "Sounder" by William H. Armstrong. Text copyright (c) 1969 by William H. Armstrong. Illustrations copyright (c) 1969 by James Barkley. Selection reprinted by permission of HarperCollins Publishers; (tr) HarperCollins; (br) From NUMBER THE STARS (JACKET COVER) by Lois Lowry. Copyright. Used by permission of Dell Books, a division of Bantam Doubleday Dell Publishing Group, Inc.; **B137:** (tl) Cover illustration by K.Thompson from THE BROCCOLI TAPES by Jan Slepian. Illustration copyright ©1990 by Scholastic Inc. Reproduced by permission of Scholastic Inc. Apple Paperbacks is a registered trademark of Scholastic Inc.; (bl) Full book cover of "Walk Two Moons" by Sharon Creech. Text copyright (c) 1994 by Sharon Creech. Selection reprinted by permission of HarperCollins Publishers.

Commissioned Illustrations

B8, B9, B24, B36, B37: Carol Richman; **B44:** Dominick Caminiti; **B82, B83, B84, B115, B116, B120, B121, B124:** S.I. International (Artists' Representative); **B115, B124:** Jordi Torres; **B56:** John Dyess

Electronic Page Makeup

Larry Rosenthal, Tom Tedesco, Dawn Annunziata, Penny Baker, Betsy Bostwick, Maude Davis, Paul DelSignore, Irene Ehrmann, Jacob Farah, Alison Grabow, Gregory Harrison, Jr., Marnie Ingman, Laura Maggio, Lynn Mandarino, David Rosenthal, Mitchell Rosenthal, Rasul Sharif, Scott Steinhardt

Administrative Services

Diane Gerard

Photo Research Service

Omni-Photo Communications, Inc.